Ghost
of a Norfolk Parson

RC priest 1995

# Ghost Stories
# of a Norfolk Parson

by
## JOHN BARNES

*Illustrated by the Author*

**MOWBRAY**
**LONDON & OXFORD**

Copyright © John Barnes 1986


First published in Mowbray's Leisure Series 1986
by A. R. Mowbray & Co. Ltd,
Saint Thomas House, Becket Street,
Oxford, OX1 1SJ

Typeset by HiTech Typesetters Ltd, Oxford
Printed in Great Britain by Cox and Wyman Ltd., Reading

**British Library Cataloguing in Publication Data**

Barnes, John
    Ghost stories of a Norfolk parson.——
    (Mowbray leisure series)
    I. Title
    823'.914 [F]   PR6052.A664/

    ISBN 0-264-67099-X

TO
THE REVEREND ALAN CAREFULL
WHOSE TELLING OF A GHOST STORY
MANY YEARS AGO
I HAVE NEVER FORGOTTEN

# Contents

# 1

# New Year's Eve

I try very hard to forget New Year's Eve, December 31st 1984, but I find it difficult. Two friends, living about twenty miles away from Wenningham, the village in Norfolk where I live and where I am parish priest, had invited me to spend the evening with them. We had a most happy time together, a good meal, good wine, and much conversation. I was sorry when it was time to leave; my friends pressed me to stay and see in the New Year with them, but as I had to be up fairly early the next morning, I said that I really ought to be getting home. And so at about half past eleven I got into my car and set off. It was a clear night, dry and frosty, and there was a full moon. The kind of night when driving is thoroughly enjoyable, and this was especially so as there was virtually no traffic on the country lanes which led towards home.

After a few miles I came to a bend in the road which in turn led on to a rather steep bridge over a river. I slowed down of course and had not yet regained speed when the car headlights picked out a youngish-looking man standing by the side of the road a little way ahead. Looking back, I feel fairly sure that he did not actually thumb a lift. But from

1

his position on the verge I imagined that it was a lift that he was hoping for, and being, I suppose, in a generous and mellow mood and aware too of the difficulty of obtaining a lift at such a time and on such a road, I stopped and opened the passenger door for the man to get in. This he did, closing the door behind him, but without speaking a word. I found this a little odd. I often give people lifts, but usually before they get into the car they ask me how far and in what direction I'm travelling. But this man didn't, and so it was left to me to inquire where it was that he wanted to go. For a moment he made no reply to my question. And then after a pause, a pause which I found somewhat unnerving, and in a voice which was at once flat, tired and hollow, he spoke the name of a village, a village which I knew to be about three miles ahead.

Now just before the car had come to a halt when I picked the man up, and when, therefore, he was plainly visible in the car lights, I had noticed that he was strangely dressed, and that he was somewhat dishevelled too. His clothes, I thought, looked very old-fashioned, almost like those worn by working-men at the end of the last century. But of course this was New Years' Eve, a night of parties, and one of my younger friends had told me only recently that fancy dress parties had made something of a come-back. So there seemed to be nothing inherently strange about the man's dress; indeed had I seen someone dressed as a knight in armour late on New Year's Eve I wouldn't have been unduly surprised. To try and make conversation I asked my passenger whether he had been to a party, but he made no answer to my question. A little further on I tried again. I commented on the brightness of the moonlight and on how the dark leafless trees stood out so clearly against the silver-grey sky. But again there was no response. This silence made me feel uncomfortable and in a strange way, even threatened. And somehow, although this is very difficult to describe and may perhaps owe something to retrospect, there was a heavy, unhappy atmosphere in the car. My passenger seemed to communicate to me a feeling of depression – even distress – which I had been very far from feeling before he had joined me. I shivered and turned the car heater higher. But despite this (and I am quite certain that this owed nothing to the imagination either at the time or subsequently) there was an unnatural coldness and still more strange, a dampness in the air.

By now we were nearing the village which the man had named, it was you remember only about three miles on from the bridge where I had picked him up. Frankly, I was glad that he would soon be leaving the car; never before had a passenger made me feel uncomfortable in the way that this man did. We reached the road sign announcing the village and then for some reason which I cannot explain I asked the man his name. It was an odd thing to do, but most of us have at some time asked a question involuntarily and maybe regretted it afterwards. I did so immediately, because there was silence and I imagined that once again the man was not going to answer the question, which in turn made me feel foolish for having asked it. But then in the same low flat tone in which he had spoken the name of the village he spoke his own name: John Lloyd. He said nothing more.

Straight afterwards (for we had, you remember, already passed the village sign) he gestured that we had reached the place where he wished to be set down. I slowed the car and almost before it had come to a stop he opened the door and leapt out, stopping neither to thank me for the lift or even to close the car door after him. I looked to see where he went and in the light of my headlights I could see that a few yards in front of the place where I had stopped there was a break in the hedge, and that in this break was set a wooden gate which appeared to lead into a church-yard. The man hurried through this gate which was, I remember, wide open and he was immediately lost in the darkness.

I felt strangely agitated and unhappy as I drove away – driving quickly, glad to be away from the place and from my passenger John Lloyd, whoever he may be. As I drove on towards home I became aware not only of the peculiar feeling of dampness which I have already mentioned, but also of a peculiar smell, which, having sniffed several times, I decided was the smell of stale water. I switched on the light inside the car and on the floor by the passenger seat there were indeed distinct pools of water. I felt the seat where the man had been sitting and found that the upholstery was soaking. This seemed extraordinary. My passenger had obviously been dripping wet and yet, as I mentioned, it was a dry

4

frosty night. I was quite certain that there had been no rain that evening, and certainly not the downpour which would have been necessary for a person's clothes to have become saturated in the way that the man's clothes clearly had been.

I got home safely, but although it was now well after midnight I found it difficult to get to sleep. I was disturbed by my experience on the road. I knew it would be difficult to get it out of my mind, and so I resolved that next day – or rather later on that same day – I would try to make some sense of the incident for my own peace of mind. The village where I had left the man was only about ten miles away and as I lay in bed I decided that I would go back there. I knew the parish priest slightly having met him once or twice at diocesan gatherings and it would be quite easy, I thought, just to call in and wish him a happy New Year. I could say that I just happened to be passing and thought I would call. And then I could ask, not immediately, whether he happened to know a person called John Lloyd. I didn't want to look silly or to admit that I had been unnerved by my experience. On the other hand, I ruminated, if this man was a stranger to the district maybe I ought to let my colleague know that someone had been about in his churchyard around midnight. It was even possible that the man might have carried out some theft, or some piece of vandalism and if so, well perhaps I could supply information which might be useful to the police. Lying there I certainly felt that I ought to do something or say something and I hoped that whatever that something was, it would serve to put my own mind at rest whether or not it proved to be helpful to the priest or police ten miles away.

We always have a celebration of the Eucharist at ten o'clock on New Year's Day and after the service I got in my car and drove over to the village where I had dropped the stranger, as I had planned. It was the loveliest kind of Winter's morning imaginable; there was a clear blue sky, and although the sunshine was bright it was not strong enough to have melted all the frost from the fields and hedges. Indeed the morning was so fresh and bright and good that I could almost have convinced myself that I had imagined the strange incident of the night before, convinced myself that it had probably been the combined result of tiredness, perhaps indigestion and even perhaps a little too much to drink. Almost, but not entirely because when I felt the upholstery of the passenger seat it was still damp, and the car floor still showed signs of wetness. But even with these indications, I still felt a little embarrassed about relating my story to a priest I hardly knew and who might well think that I was making a fuss about something quite trivial. So when I reached the village it was easy to decide that before I actually went to the vicarage I would first have a look at the church and churchyard.

I drew up outside the church gate just as I had done not twelve hours earlier and there I had my first surprise of the morning. Last night, in the light of the car headlights, I was quite sure that the entrance to the churchyard, the entrance through which the man had passed, had been a fairly simple wooden gate, the kind of oak gate which leads into many country

6

churchyards in rural Norfolk. But now I could see the entrance was quite different; access to the church-yard was gained by a rather handsome lych-gate built of flints and stone and with a lead-covered roof. Architecture is one of my interests and I could guess that this gateway had been constructed somewhere around the turn of the century. Indeed as I passed through it I read an inscription, carved in stone on one of the side-walls recording that it had been built in 1903 in memory of a former Vicar. I was puzzled over the gateway, but it had certainly been dark the night before and obviously I had been mistaken in thinking that there was only a simple wooden gate there. Yet I was unconvinced, puzzled and again uneasy.

Be that as it may, I entered the yard as my passenger had done and walked up the well-kept gravel path which led from the gateway to the church porch. I walked slowly enjoying the morning, the sparkle of sunlight on the frosty grass and the long shadows cast by the dark yew trees planted along the boundary. My feet crunched on the gravel and as I walked I looked at the finely carved headstones dating from the eighteenth and nineteenth-centuries, which are such a feature of our Norfolk churchyards. As I neared the porch my eye lighted on one stone in particular, a stone which stood out somewhat be-cause it was not encrusted with litchens as the others were. It somehow looked new and yet it obviously was not new. I glanced at the inscription on it and as I read its few words I felt chilled, despite the bright winter sunshine. The words I read were these:

JOHN LLOYD

DIED BY DROWNING

DECEMBER 31st 1884

AGED 23

I did not call at the Vicarage. And never again will I
drive down that particular country road on a New
Year's Eve.

# 2

# Highgrove

In Saxon times, the village of Wenningham (at that time, I imagine, little more than a group of huts) lay just south of the parish church. Then through the centuries, it crept first to the West and then to the North so that now only three houses stand where the original village stood. One of these is the old brick house which is built at the foot of the steps leading up into the churchyard. One is the modern rectory standing in a group of beech and sycamore trees some two or three hundred yards away and the third is a long low farmhouse, Priory Farm, a similar distance beyond the rectory and surrounded by its various barns and outbuildings.

But until 1851 there was another house in this quiet corner of the village. It was called Highgrove and it stood on a site roughly equidistant from the farm and the site of the present rectory. Nothing remains of it now except for its cellars, which are no more than walls and holes in the ground, covered in summer by nettles and briars and surrounded by a fence to prevent animals and children from falling in. Shaded by the copse of trees which lies between the farm and the rectory, these remains of Highgrove have about them that desolate and unhappy feeling which one so often senses at the site of a demolished house. Certainly, knowing what I do now, I sense that desolation very strongly and I usually avoid passing the remains of Highgrove when I set out across the fields for my Sunday afternoon walk.

I have seen a couple of engravings of the house (which had disappeared, of course, before the age of photography) and also a sketch, carefully drawn in red ink which is kept in an album at the Priory, our local 'big-house'. From the pictures Highgrove appears to have been a fairly large house dating from the middle of the eighteenth century, in size somewhere between a good Norfolk farmhouse and the house of a country landowner. It appears, moreover, to have been an attractive house and certainly it had been built in a fine position, standing on a slight rise and looking south along the shallow valley in which the village of Wenningham stands. So it seemed strange to me that this handsome house should have been demolished when it was barely a century old and at a time when large families and domestic labour were both plentiful. If it had not been required for use by a member of the Calthorpe family at the Priory, well surely it could have been let? What, I wondered, could have led Daniel Calthorpe (whom I deduced must have been the squire in 1851) to demolish Highgrove? It seemed most curious. But I only entertained these thoughts in an idle way; I did not bother to try and find any further information, either about the house or about its untimely end. When I did discover the solution to this puzzle it was entirely by accident and it happened like this.

About two years ago I decided to write a new guide book for our parish church, the old one was out of stock and out of date so it seemed best to re-write it rather than to just revise it. I knew that the church had undergone a restoration by a well-known Victorian architect sometime in the late 1860s and that the principal benefactor had been Henry Calthorpe, son of the Daniel Calthorpe mentioned above. I wanted to discover more about this restoration and since we had no information about it whatsoever in our parish records, I decided that the best thing might be to consult the Calthorpe papers which I knew to have been deposited in the Norfolk Records Office at Norwich. So, on my next day off, I went to Norwich armed with pencil and paper. I filled in the necessary request form and a few minutes later the family papers were produced, contained in no less than five large cardboard boxes. Somewhat daunted, I began to wade through them. To be brief, I never did find the information that I was looking for about the restoration of the church. But I did, much to my surprise, stumble upon the tragic and extraordinary circumstances which led to the demolition of Highgrove House.

Amongst the papers were a bundle of letters written to Mrs Daniel Calthorpe of Wenningham Priory by her eldest daughter, Charlotte. Charlotte had married a clergyman, the Reverend John Lee, and was living in Hampshire. What I found myself reading was, of course, only one side of the correspondence. Whether Mrs Calthorpe's letters survive I don't know; certainly they do not form part of the collection of family papers deposited at Norwich. From Charlotte's letters however (which I began to read initially because they were written in a particularly neat and legible hand) a clear picture emerged, and this, without actually quoting the letters which I did not transcribe, I will try to summarise.

Almost all of the letters dealt largely with one Harriet. At first I thought that she must be a sister of Charlotte but I soon realised that they were in fact cousins. Harriet, it appeared, had been orphaned as a child and had been brought up at the Priory with Charlotte, Henry and their other younger brothers. It was obvious from the letters that she had been a great favourite with the family and especially with her uncle, Daniel Calthorpe. It seemed that Harriet had made an ill-advised and unhappy marriage with the younger son of another old Norfolk family, a man called George Walpole. He emerges from the letters as a worthless character, drinking heavily, gambling and spending much of the time with friends of a similar mind in Norwich or London. He was also guilty, the family suspected, of using both mental and even physical cruelty towards his wife. Happily, there were no children by the marriage. Harriet was loyal to her husband and the letters give the impression that the family was sometimes irritated by her refusal to hear or speak ill of him. Because of the life he led Walpole was hardly able to support his wife and for that reason (and so that the family might be able to give Harriet whatever support and comfort they could) Daniel Calthorpe had given Walpole the tenancy of Highgrove House on the Wenningham estate.

Early in 1851 matters seem to have come to a head. Daniel could no longer tolerate the situation; the Calthorpes considered that Walpole was becoming increasingly degenerate, and they consulted between themselves as to what could best be done. Charlotte was included in the consultations and her letters to her mother provide an indirect account of what transpired. They decided that the marriage must be brought to an end and in the hope of achieving this Walpole's tenancy of Highgrove was to be terminated. Whereupon, the family hoped, Harriet would return to the Priory whilst her penniless husband would go, like the devil, to his own place. There is nothing in the letters to suggest that Harriet herself had been consulted or even informed of all this, but be that as it may, before the next quarter day notice to vacate Highgrove had been served upon George Walpole. As regards his reaction to this news all that is known from the letters is that the family were incensed to learn that invitations had been issued for a large party to be held at Highgrove just a few days before the tenancy was due to end. True to form George Walpole had clearly decided to leave with a defiant flourish and the Calthorpes gathered that a great many people had been summoned to this strange celebration, most of them drawn from what Charlotte referred to contemptuously as 'the scum of Norfolk society'.

After the two or three letters in which this development is commented upon, the next in the series, together with those which follow it, are written on black-edged notepaper and the events to which they refer are these. The party which George Walpole had planned at Highgrove duly took place and Harriet, much one imagines against her inclination and will, took her place as hostess for the last time in her marital home. The party, as her relatives had forecast, became rowdy and profane as the guests, encouraged by their host, became increasingly drunk and noisy. Towards midnight, nauseated by what she had heard and seen Harriet began to make her way up the main staircase to her room. Walpole saw her leaving the party and in drunken anger over the insult which his muddled brain considered she was offering to his guests he stumbled up the stairs after her. At the head of the staircase he seized her by the shoulders and pushed her back roughly towards the wild scene below. She fell awkwardly and in falling she broke her neck. At the inquest which was held subsequently the opinion was given that she had died instantly.

Those black-edged letters which Charlotte Lee wrote to her mother in the following weeks reflect accurately, I imagine, the mingled outrage and grief which the whole Calthorpe family felt. They depict too the full approval which the family gave to Daniel Calthorpe's decision to demolish Highgrove. Never again, he had apparently vowed, would a member of his family or any other person live in that unhappy house where his niece had suffered so much and where, as he maintained, she had finally been murdered. Never again, he said, would there be laughter on that spot which had resounded with the mirth of Walpole's debauched friends on that fateful night. And so, it appears from the letters, the order was given. In a matter of weeks the builders from the estate yard had moved in and become demolition men. The fine house, its roof, its walls, its fireplaces and plasterwork, its elegant staircase – all these were systematically hacked down and destroyed. The Agent suggested, it seems, that at least the doors and window frames might be stored at the estate yard for future use. But Daniel Calthorpe rejected the idea. No, nothing must remain above ground.

Yet although Highgrove House was erased, reduced to those low weed-covered walls and gaping cellars which are all that remain of it today, Daniel Calthorpe didn't, I believe, fully achieve his intention that never again should there be sounds of laughter heard on that unhappy spot. I happen to sleep on that side of the new Rectory which faces towards the site where Highgrove once stood and its remains, as I indicated earlier, are in a group of trees just a few hundred yards away from my window. Sometimes on a windy night when the clouds scud across the sky, obscuring for a time the brightness of the moon and when the wind roars and moans in the beech and sycamore trees, I feel sure that I can hear the sounds of music and laughter. And then – but maybe I imagine it – a scream, and after that, silence . . .

# 3

# The Third Bell

I had not heard about the tragedy of Joseph Turner when I first took up bell-ringing. I suppose it was one of those skeletons in the parish cupboard which tend not to be communicated to newcomers, but which at some later date are eventually revealed in hushed tones. However, when I finally did hear the story, it was this.

In the first two decades of this century, Wenningham, like so many other country villages, had a strong band of church bell ringers. There were relatively few other forms of amusement and recreation in those days and bell-ringing offered an acceptable combination of fellowship together with physical and mental exercise. Several times each year, apparently, the ringers would attempt to ring a peal, a feat which takes about three hours to perform and an immense expenditure of concentration and energy. Sometimes the peal would be achieved and sometimes not. But towards the year 1920 the number of times when the complicated pattern of striking which makes up a peal, broke down and the peal was lost, had noticeably increased. The reason for this, it seems, was Joseph Turner. In his day he had been a fine ringer, well-known in bell-ringing circles throughout the diocese. But now he was quite simply getting past it. On too many occasions he had become exhausted and confused when the peal had been going for about an hour, and the correct order of striking had been lost and the peal had had to be abandoned. His fellow ringers, most of whom had been ringing with him for a good number of years, were very loyal but understandably resentment began to grow. It was generally felt, although for a long time it was unspoken, that he ought to know himself when it was time to give up and hand over the third bell (which was the one he usually rang) to one of the promising young lads whom the band had been training.

Then in 1920 it was learned that the parish priest of Wenningham, Father Reeves, was going to retire. He had been Rector for about sixteen years and was very popular, not least with the band of ringers. He would often join them at the Red Lion for a drink after their weekly practice on Thursday evenings, something which in those days was rather unusual. He had also established a tradition of giving the ringers and their wives an annual party at the rectory just after Christmas and this too had always been appreciated and enjoyed. So the news of his impending departure from the village was received with regret and the ringers decided to pay him the traditional compliment of a farewell peal rung in his honour. This decision was made one Thursday evening when the band was having its usual drink and it so happened that on that occasion neither Joseph Turner nor Father Reeves himself were present. Once the decision to ring the complimentary peal was made, and the date fixed, one of the younger ringers voiced the question which was on everyone's mind: was it wise to let Joseph Turner form part of the team for the peal? Wouldn't it be both unfortunate and embarrassing for a complimentary peal to fail? And if Joseph Turner was included, as he always had been in the past, was it not tantamount to inviting failure?

After some discussion they unwillingly reached the decision that one of the young men they had been training should be asked to handle the third bell. Arrangements were made and I suppose that one of the senior ringers should have volunteered to go and explain the position to Joseph Turner, but no one was willing to take on such a difficult job and so nothing was done. Extraordinarily in a village like ours, Turner didn't find out that the peal was to be attempted and so the first thing he heard about it came from the bells themselves when they were rung-up one Saturday afternoon and the peal began. He was in his garden at the time and already somewhat breathless through the exertion of digging. He was far from young and certainly was not as fit as he had been. Whether or not he realised why the peal was being rung no one knows, he knew only too well, however, that a peal was beginning and that he had been excluded from it. In an almost blind fury, he was seen by a neighbour to throw his spade down and run headlong out of his garden gate and down the village street towards the church. Whether his intention was to seize the third bell from the hands of the man who was ringing it, or merely to register an angry protest, again no one knows and maybe he did not know himself. The fact is that he reached the church, entered the little door beneath the tower, and began to climb up the stone steps leading to the ringing-chamber. But he never reached it. The ringers above heard the sound of feet coming up the spiral staircase, they heard too the heavy, laboured breathing. Halfway up, he collapsed. His heart, it was supposed, having given way under the combined strain of the digging, running and climbing and perhaps above all, the anger. The footsteps stopped, there was a groan and then a moment later a thudding and scraping sound as his body fell backwards. It may, perhaps, have been of some satisfaction to him that, for this last time, he caused the failure of the peal that was being attempted on that Saturday afternoon.

Well I knew nothing of all this in my early days at Wenningham. It had taken place more than half a century before and country people are not quick to tell people about their parish skeletons. As a new parish priest I was anxious to show interest in the various parish activities and so like Father Reeves before me I began to join the bell ringers for their weekly drink after bell-practice. After two or three weeks, when they had got to know me, they said why didn't I come along to the practice itself sometime? Could I handle a bell? No? – well they would teach me if I wanted. It was something they said that a parson should know about and I was inclined to agree. So I went along the following week, climbing the stone stairs up to the ringing chamber and I continued to do so week by week until I had made reasonable progress. It is usual, understandably, for beginners to be taught on one of the lighter bells which are the easier ones to handle and so it was either the treble, second or third bells which I found myself ringing – with increasing confidence – at the weekly practices.

The ropes in a ringing-chamber are arranged roughly in a circle and the ringers stand before them with their backs to the walls of the tower, facing inwards. That way you can see what everyone else is doing and thereby (hopefully) you ring in concert. It so happens that in our tower the rope attached to the third bell comes down in front of the doorway leading into the ringing-chamber from the stone spiral staircase, so that whoever rings that bell stands with his back to the doorway. Often as a novice I found myself in that position, ringing the third bell. And everytime I did so I had a peculiar sensation. I heard, or at least I thought I heard, the sound of footsteps coming up the stone steps behind me. The sound was quite unmistakable and each time I heard the footsteps coming I turned my head slightly, naturally, involuntarily, expecting to see someone appear. But no one ever did, because the footsteps always seemed to stop before they got to the head of the stairs and reached the low doorway into the chamber.

I think, looking back, that the other ringers must have noticed that my head turned towards the doorway from time to time, but they certainly did not comment upon it. I too said nothing, because it really

23

sounded rather foolish. Each time it happened I tried to explain it away, although the explanations which I produced for myself never struck me as very convincing. Perhaps, I thought to myself, it was rope-rattle, or maybe the slight movement of the other ringers' feet on the wooden floor. But the sound of feet ascending a stone staircase is a distinctive sound and I was really quite sure that this was what I kept hearing: footsteps which never reached the top of the stairs.

When I had been ringing for some weeks, the Captain of the tower told us that he had received a letter from a band of ringers at Norwich, asking if they could include our tower in an outing which they were planning to our part of the county. This is something which happens from time to time, I suppose bands of ringers tend to include our bells in their tours because they have the reputation of having a particularly sweet tone. The day came and some of us went along to welcome the visitors and to watch them for a while. Now as well as the ringing-boards and the faded group-photographs of parish bands in past generations, our ringing-chamber is also furnished with wooden benches which run around three of its sides. It so happened that I sat down, not deliberately, on the side opposite the doorway on to the stone staircase and therefore opposite to the visiting ringer who was handling the third bell. It had not been my intention to watch him, but from where I found myself sitting it was inevitable that I should do so. And I could hardly fail to notice that, just like myself when ringing that particular bell, he several times half-turned his head, as if expecting someone to come in through the doorway into the chamber. But no one came. I was fascinated, and could not take my eyes off him. It was quite obvious that he was hearing the same sound: the sound of footsteps coming up the stairs, but never reaching the top.

I now felt sure that the sounds which I seemed to hear every time I rang that third bell were not a figment of my imagination. And I decided that when I had my next after-practice drink with the ringers I would mention it – quite casually – and see if there was any reaction. This I did. I told them what I had heard myself and by way of corroboration I told them that I had seen just the same thing happening when the Norwich ringers had been in the tower. They glanced at one another and then after a pause one of them told me the story of Joseph Turner which I have just recounted. 'But,' he added neither you nor that ringer from Norwich had ever heard the story, so both of you were able to hear old Joseph coming up. It's a queer thing, but once someone knows about it, knows what happened on that Saturday afternoon back in 1920, then he never hears the footsteps again. Don't know why, but that's how it is.' Which, I have discovered, is true. For although I have rung the third bell many times since, never again have I heard those mysterious footsteps ascending up and up towards the ringing-chamber, but never reaching it.

# 4

# The Smell of Tobacco

I told one or two people about something which happened on St. Luke's Day, October 18th, a couple of years ago and they showed no interest whatsoever, if anything, they were inclined to laugh at it. So I am rather loath to tell the story again. But whilst it may be very trivial, it struck me as being so strange that I think I ought to record it.

Our parish church in Wenningham stands on the edge of the village and is built on a slight bank. Outside the main West doorway there is a short paved path and then a flight of stone steps which leads down into Church Street. Church Street is only, I suppose, three or four hundred yards long and at the far end it issues onto the High Street. At that far end there are a few estate cottages. Nearer to the church the River Stewkey and a piece of swampy land lie on one side and on the other there is the brick wall which encloses the grounds of Wenningham priory. The wall is about eight feet high and behind it is a narrow belt of woodland which, together with the wall itself, shelters the gardens of the priory from the road.

The October 18th of which I am speaking happened to be a Tuesday and it was a perfect

Autumn morning. The sun shone from a deep blue sky and the leaves of the chestnut trees were bright yellow, the odd one floating lazily down onto the road. There was that particular feeling in the air, at once both damp and crisp, which makes mid-Autumn one of the most attractive times of the year. There was certainly nothing at all to suggest that anything strange, anything out of the ordinary might be about to happen. Except, perhaps, for the fact that there was an extraordinary stillness in the air. Indeed it was this stillness, something altogether more intense than the mere absence of noise and movement, which impressed me as I walked out of the church, down the steps, and out into Church Street on that bright October morning. Usually as one walks down the street mid-morning a car passes, or one meets someone out with their dog or someone making their way either to the shops or to the churchyard. But on this occasion there was complete silence – no vehicles, no people, no animals. Complete stillness.

Then, as I walked along beneath the priory wall, heading towards the High Street, I suddenly became aware of a strong and quite distinct smell of tobacco. I don't smoke myself and so like all non-smokers I am very sensitive to this particular smell. It was quite unmistakable; it was not the smell of cigarette smoke, or the smoke from a cigar. It was quite definitely the smell of a pipe being smoked. I stopped and sniffed several times. Where could the smoke be coming from? There was no one at all in the street, it was completely deserted. So far as I could tell no one had passed the spot recently and anyhow the smell

28

was far too distinct to have been hanging about since someone passed the spot earlier. I was both intrigued and perplexed. The only possible explanation that I could think of was that one of the gardeners or woodmen on the estate had wandered into the belt of trees bordering the wall in order to have a smoke. But this seemed unlikely, especially as it happened to be about 10.30 am, a time when I knew that the men working in the grounds were always ensconced in the kitchen at the priory, being regaled with cups of tea by the cook-housekeeper. Or perhaps, I thought, some boy out of the village had given himself a day off school and had shinned over the wall in order to have an undetected smoke. But this too did not seem very likely, especially as the smoke which I could smell so distinctly was quite definitely coming from a pipe, not a cigarette.

I was so intrigued by this that I slipped back to the church steps, and since no one was about I clambered up onto one of the flat-topped gate-posts which stand at the head of the steps. Standing on this vantage point I could get a fairly clear view, obstructed only by a few branches, into the area immediately behind the priory wall. But so far as I could see there was no one there, gardener, schoolboy, or anyone else, either smoking a pipe or otherwise. Baffled, I slid down from the gatepost thankful that no one had seen me in such a curious position. A moment later a car turned into the street, a woman pushing a pram appeared, and that strange stillness was broken. Life returned to normal and when going down the street again I reached the place where only a few minutes

29

before the smell of tobacco had been so strong, I found that all trace of it was now gone. There seemed to be no possible explanation. So I got on with what I was doing, and for the time being forgot completely about this odd incident.

That afternoon I did some routine parish visiting. One of the people on my list was a lady well on in her seventies, who lived in the same small cottage in which she had been born, something quite usual in the past but now, with rehousing and a mobile society, something to be commented upon. Over a cup of tea we talked as we often had before about life as it had been in Wenningham in the first half of the century. I find that older people like talking about things as they were in the days of their childhood and youth, and I, for my part, never tire of hearing about that whole way of life which has now passed and yet which is still so firmly present in living memory. On this occasion we got on to the subject of the last Calthorpe squire, Henry James Calthorpe, who died unmarried in 1916, the last of a family which had owned the Wenningham estate for nearly three-hundred years. He was the grandson of the Daniel Calthorpe mentioned in an earlier story. 'What a character he was!' the old lady reminisced. 'He always wore a Tam O'Shanter hat, and during the summer he used to play bowls on the priory lawn – he loved playing bowls. But he was really eccentric, especially in the last few years of his life. He was very shy, too, and must have been a bit lonely. You never saw him out in the street. Hardly ever left the priory grounds. We children were a bit afraid of him really.

And when we went down Church Street on the way to Catechism, he'd often be behind the wall, and he'd throw boiled sweets over it for us to catch! Sometimes he'd be there and sometimes he wouldn't. Of course we couldn't see him, because he was behind the wall, but I suppose he'd hear us going past. But we always knew whether he was there, . . . we could smell the smoke from his pipe. Yes, he was a great smoker . . . never without his pipe, except in church . . .' Immediately, of course, I recalled my odd experience that morning, and I felt a shiver go down my back. I suspected that I had learned the source of that unaccountable smell of tobacco smoke. But I said nothing.

Evensong is said in church at seven o'clock each day, and that evening I made a point of arriving in the sacristy a few minutes earlier than usual. There was something I wanted to look up. I unlocked the safe in which we keep our old church registers, and I got out the burial register which records burials in the churchyard up to the year 1918, when the present register was begun. I went backwards starting from a burial which had taken place on December 28th, 1916. December 11th, . . . November 15th . . . November 2nd . . . – yes, here was the entry that I was looking for: Henry James Calthorpe, of Wenningham Priory, who died on October 18th, 1916. It was as I had imagined, today was the anniversary of the last squire's death.

# 5

# The South Calke Road

'There is a lovely road that runs from Ixopo into the hills' – those, if I remember rightly, are the opening words of Alan Paton's famous novel *Cry, the Beloved Country* and they often come into my mind when I drive from our village of Wenningham to the neighbouring village of South Calke, some five and a half miles away. Because the road which links them is indeed a lovely road, running over a piece of higher ground which separates the shallow valleys in which the two villages lie. There are certain points on this road (it would really be more accurate to call it a lane) at which fine views over rolling countryside open up. Other parts of the road are bordered by woodland, but for the most part there are simply verges, hedgerows and behind them large fields used for arable farming. In early summer the verges are white with a froth of Our-Lady's-Lace, and then a few weeks later the dog roses are out and after them the poppies. The hedgerows are punctuated by less-than-shapely oak trees, and are hung in autumn with a mass of glossy hawthorn berries; in high Summer the fields beyond are pale golden with acre upon acre of barley and wheat, stretching onwards towards the vast pale-blue East Anglian sky.

A lovely road, and an unusually quiet one, even by Norfolk standards. More often than not it is possible to drive the five and a half miles without meeting a single vehicle. Quiet too because there are so few buildings along it. Soon after leaving Wenningham you pass a small group of estate cottages, known as the 'pink cottages' because of the colour of their walls. Then half a mile on from them a ruined church stands alone in a meadow and then finally, about half way between the two villages there is a crossroads, merely the intersection of two country lanes and at the crossroads there is one isolated cottage, surrounded by a patch of rough ground which is presided over by a very noisy family of geese.

I know the South Calke road well and I always used to enjoy driving along it. So when I heard it mentioned one evening when some of the members of our Church Men's Group were having a drink together at the Red Lion, following their monthly meeting, I pricked my ears up. I do not know how the road had come up in the conversation, but I heard one of the men, Bill Green – a very sensible early to middle-aged man, who works as a Representative for a firm of agricultural engineers – I heard him say quietly 'well I certainly wouldn't drive along that road at night . . . there's something very odd about it'. I was quite taken aback by this remark, but I knew somehow not to follow it up. He had clearly said all that he intended to say and it was noticeable that no one else in the group of village men questioned or challenged what he had said.

As I lay in bed that night, I turned that chance remark over in my mind. I was intrigued by it. What could be odd about the South Calke road, that quiet lane running through such charming countryside? Whatever could have given it a bad reputation amongst local people? In my ruminations, I decided (really for no good reason) that if some strange or violent event had left some kind of mark upon that area, it was most probably something to do with the ruined church, for a ruined church seemed to be obvious and excellent material for a manifestation of the supernatural. Then I realised that although I am fairly interested in local history, and certainly in ancient buildings, I really knew nothing at all about this particular ruined building, standing alone on a rise, and with little of it remaining other than the tower, invariably the last part of an old church to collapse, and in this case standing almost to its full height. So I did a little research in the course of the next few days and I was able to pick up at least a few facts about the building and its history. The church and manor, I found, had belonged to the great Cathedral Priory of Norwich before the Reformation, and at the Dissolution of the Monasteries, that great seizure and plunder of monastic lands, it had been acquired by a courtier, Sir Nicholas Bradshaw. By the early years of the sixteenth century, apparently, the small village around the church had already been in decline, and Bradshaw simply finished off what time had begun. The priest who had served the small church on behalf of the priory was dismissed and the building was turned into a barn to serve the fields around it. Here, it seemed, was the kind of information I had been looking for and expecting. My imagination got to work on it, and when using the South Calke road, as I did on a number of occasions in the ensuing Spring and early Summer, I quite expected to encounter the ghostly figure of the priest as he wandered away from his former charge, homeless and destitute. And if he did not appear, though he seemed to be by far the most likely candidate, then I was equally prepared to meet up with either a group of dispossessed monks, intoning some solemn dirge, or else with the ruthless and impious Sir Nicholas himself, condemned to ride for ever over the church lands which he had acquired and despoiled.

So when driving along that road from South Calke at dusk one August evening, I saw walking ahead of me the figure of a clergyman who obviously belonged to no other century than our own, I did not feel any alarm or excitement. (I should explain that North Norfolk is a popular area for holidays and so there is nothing odd about strangers, clerical or lay, walking the lanes on a Summer evening.) I slowed down, as I had often done in similar circumstances, opened the passenger door and called out 'Would you like a lift, Father? I'm driving down into Wenningham'. And in he got. I suppose it was about nine o'clock on that mid-August evening. It was, as I mentioned before, just getting dusk, but I still only had the side-lights of the car on, and so I didn't get a clear view of the priest's face. As soon as he got in, however, I was immediately aware that he was in a very agitated state. He seemed 'worked-up' as we say; tense, perhaps fearful. Rather as if he was either in a hurry to get away from somewhere or else in a hurry to get somewhere else. I said 'Are you making for Wenningham, Father?', and he replied breathlessly 'Yes . . . Yes, . . . straight on, straight on . . .' As we drove away from the spot where I had picked him up, it was his strange tenseness which I was most aware of; he seemed to be holding on the sides of his seat, sitting very upright and peering forward to the road ahead of us. Needless to say I found this behaviour, and his whole manner, quite unnerving. Straightaway I became agitated myself, his tenseness communicated itself to me. I felt as if something untoward was about to happen or appear.

I suppose it was because of my own discomfort in this atmosphere that I did not address any further remark to him in the next minute or so. The more especially because I felt that this tension, which I find so difficult to describe, was mounting. Not more than a quarter of a mile ahead of the place where I had picked the priest up – which was on that section of the road which is bordered by woodland – lay the crossroads, the crossroads where, you remember, there is an isolated cottage, guarded in daytime by geese. I was still, I realise now, accelerating after having stopped to pick the priest up. We had the right of way at the crossroads (not that rights of way mattered much in these quiet country lanes, where one so rarely meets another vehicle) and so there was no cause for me to slow down. We reached the crossroads, no, we were on it, when without warning the priest let out the most terrible – and terrifying – cry.

A sound somewhere between a scream and a shout. I cannot describe it. But I can still, in my mind, hear it, and indeed I sometimes do still hear it in nightmares. For the first time, I suppose, I knew what the odd expression 'blood-curdling' means.

Now beside other things, telling you this story involves me in confessing that I am a nervous, even jumpy, driver. And that I live, secretly, in fear of having a serious collision with some vehicle which I have through negligence failed to see. So when my passenger let out that awful cry, my immediate reaction was to assume that another car was coming out of one of those side roads which make up the crossroads, and that I had not seen it. Perhaps a less nervous and more capable driver than I am, finding himself in this position and making the same supposition that I had made, would have accelerated out of the situation. But that was not my reaction. My natural reaction in that split-second was to slam on the brakes. And that is what I did. The car came to a violent halt just beyond the crossroads and of course the engine stalled. I think I must have been shaking like the proverbial leaf when, after I suppose only a few seconds, I pulled myself together and took stock of the situation. It had been a nasty shock. But two things began to dawn upon me. One was the fact that no other vehicle of any description had been involved. So far as I could tell, and I think I could tell with perfect accuracy, all four roads leading on to the crossroads were completely empty apart from my own car. The other thing was the state of my companion. He was doubled up in the passenger seat, his head nearly on his knees, completely motionless. Later, I was surprised that he had not hit his head on the windscreen and perhaps broken it, since he had not been wearing a seat-belt, as I had been doing. But this did not occur to me immediately. My feeling, maybe from intuition, or maybe based squarely upon the fact that the man was motionless and made no response to either my words or my touch, was that he was dead. Whichever, the fact is that I panicked. I jumped out of the car (leaving it just where it had stopped in the middle of the road) feeling that I must go and fetch help.

Now the isolated cottage by the crossroads was no more than a hundred yards away and I could see that its living-room window was lit up, the lighted window shining in the gathering dusk. I ran in through the wicket gate, down the short path and up to the door; dogs barked as I approached and somehow that normal sound was reassuring after the terrible cry of the priest and the scream of the car-tyres. I knocked loudly and rapidly on the door and as there was no immediate response I knocked again. Then there was a shuffle of elderly feet, and an old man, backed by his two barking dogs, cautiously opened the door a little and then, seeing my clerical collar and becoming aware, perhaps, of my distress, he opened it wider. His wife now came up behind him, craning forward to see who it was and what was the matter. It was he who spoke first, for despite that fact that I had run only a few yards I was breathless. In answer to his inquiry I explained as best I could that there had been an accident – no, it had not really been an accident . . . I had given a priest a lift . . . picked him up not long before the crossroads . . . had stopped suddenly, thought I was going to hit something . . . and the priest . . . the stop seemed to have brought on some sort of attack . . . he was doubled up . . . seemed in a bad way . . .

As I tried to explain what was the matter, I was aware that the story I was telling was causing considerable distress to the man's wife. She turned very pale, put her hands to her face, and repeated the words 'not again, . . . not again'. The man, however, remained calm. 'I'll come with you', he said, and picked up a strong torch. As we left the cottage I said 'I'm so sorry about this . . . so sorry to have upset your wife . . . I didn't think about that.' 'Well,' he replied, 'It's just that there was a bad accident on this crossroads oh, about twenty years ago, a priest was killed then and whenever the wife gets reminded of it, it makes her upset. It's not your fault.' A moment later we were at the car. It was now almost dark, and we needed the old man's torch. I admit I was fearful as we opened the passenger door. The old man shone his torch into the car . . . and yes, it was empty. There was no one in the passenger seat. The car was empty, and the road was empty too; the man from the cottage shone his powerful torch down each of the four lanes, but there was no sound or sight of anyone at all on that still August night.

I did not know what to say, or indeed what to think. I was too shattered to feel foolish and there was no explanation to be given. I was just drained and speechless. The old man too, just a shape in the gathering night, stood there and said nothing, whilst his wife, who had followed us, stood a few yards away, sobbing quietly. Indeed, there was nothing that could be said except, perhaps, for the words spoken by Bill Green in the Red Lion some months before: 'There's something very strange about that South Calke road . . .'

# 6

# The Two 'Cellists

About one hundred years ago there was a rather distinguished Rector of Wenningham. His name was George Ratcliffe Woodward and in the course of his long life he composed a considerable number of carols and edited several carol books. I suppose the carol of his which most people have heard of is *Ding Dong! Merrily on High*, which has become an established part of the Christmas repertoire. He was Rector here for just six years, most of the remainder of his life being spent in London where he devoted his time to carol-writing and historical studies, but when he died as an old man in 1934 his body was brought back to Wenningham for burial and it lies in the churchyard just outside the little Priest's Door in the South wall of the Chancel.

Father Woodward was offered the living of Wenningham in 1882 by the then squire, Henry Calthorpe, son of Daniel Calthorpe and father of Henry James Calthorpe, both of whom we have encountered already. These three men, together with other members of the family who lived here during the three centuries when the Calthorpe's were lords of the manor, lie buried in the family vault under the Chancel itself. I had often puzzled how it was that a fairly elderly Norfolk landowner should have chosen as parish priest a young London curate who was known for his extreme high-church practices and opinions – for such Father Woodward was. But when, attracted by Woodward's life, work and character I started to do some research (having the writing of a short memoire in mind) I found that there was something – something rather unusual – which linked the two men. It was not, as I had been told, that they were distantly related; I was able to prove that this was not true. No, it was the fact that Woodward and Calthorpe were both of them keen amateur cellists. Furthermore, I discovered that both of them used to bring their cellos to church with them, and use them to accompany the daily services of Mattins and Evensong! A hundred years ago it must have been very unusual for a country church to have daily sung services, but for those services to have been accompanied by two cellos must have made Wenningham unique in Christendom! In the days before the events I am about to relate, I had often thought how much I should have liked to hear one of those services, because like so many other people I think that the cello is one of the most beautiful of musical instruments and when played in a resonant building such as our parish church here, it casts a spell which most people who appreciate music find difficult to resist.

One Friday evening in late Autumn I had returned home after doing some visiting a little before nine o'clock. I had put some supper on a tray and placed myself in front of the television set. Whereupon, as happens not infrequently in a Rectory, the telephone rang, and with as good a grace as possible I put my tray down and went to answer it. It was my next-door neighbour, John Lester, who lives in the old house built opposite the steps leading up to the church gate. He wondered, he said, whether there was anything going on in church? Not, I said, so far as I knew. Why? Well, he said, he had just arrived home from a business trip, had parked his car outside his house and then as he had walked towards his front door he was quite sure that he had heard music coming from the church. He thought perhaps he ought to check with me that everything was alright. I said that I was sure it was. The organist has a key of course and quite often he practices in the evening. He prefers, he says, to play when people are not walking about. So it must be him I said. Nothing to worry about, but thank you very much for phoning to check. A speedy return I thought, to my supper and the Nine o'clock News. But no. John said that he did not think that it was the organist practicing. For one thing the church was in total darkness and for another the sound that he had heard – yes, he was quite certain that he had heard it – did not sound at all like an organ.

There was nothing for it. My supper and the news were abandoned, a coat was thrown on, a flashlight picked up, and down the drive I trudged through the wet, blustery night. John met me outside the church door, he agreed that he could hear nothing now and neither could I. Nevertheless I turned the big iron key in the lock, causing the customary crash and rattle; we put all the lights on and had a thorough look around. Nothing was out of place and certainly there was nothing to be heard. I was, I admit, more than a little sceptical about John's story. Maybe he had heard music, but I doubted very much whether it had come from the church. I wondered whether his teenage-daughter might have been playing a record in her room upstairs just at the moment when he arrived home and walked up the path? Or again, Friday night is Youth Club evening and I thought that maybe the sounds of pop music being played had been carried down from the Parish Hall on the wind. It is amazing how sound can carry and what tricks a sudden change in the direction of the wind can play. Or yet again, the sounds that he had heard could possibly have been nothing more than the wind itself, soughing and sighing in the row of tall Scots pine trees which grow along the boundary wall of the churchyard and which murmur in even the slightest wind. By the time we had locked up again, I sensed that even John himself was beginning to wonder whether he really had heard music coming from the dark, locked church. I went home, caught the final news headlines, and forgot all about the incident.

Until, that is, the following Friday. Once again I was eating my supper at about nine o'clock when the telephone rang, I answered it and found that it was my other neighbour, Tom Morton from Priory Farm – the farm which lies just a few hundred hards from the church and the rectory. He told me that a few minutes before he had gone across the yard to one of his outbuildings – he had forgotten to do something or to fetch something, I cannot remember now. Anyhow, he said that he had glanced towards the church, which lies slightly below the farm, and through the clear glass of the windows which in day-time flood the church with light, he could see a faint glow. At first he had not been quite sure about it, he had wondered whether it could be a reflection from the lights in his yard, so rather than trouble me he had kindly gone across the churchyard and looked in. There he had seen quite clearly, for the windows are not only clear but reasonably low, that the six tall candles on the Altar were alight. And also, he added, he could hear some music. 'Organ music?', I asked. 'Oh no', he replied, 'it didn't sound a bit like the organ. Well really it was like a couple of violins, only played much lower'. At that moment I remembered, of course, what had happened on the previous Friday and I also felt a slight shiver go down my back. 'Can you come across to church?' I asked him. He said he would and a few minutes later the big key crashed and rattled in the lock once again. The church was now in total darkness but a moment later the electric lights illuminated it brightly and we walked up the nave and into the chancel. Tom was incredulous that the altar candles were now unlit and I think both of us were disturbed by the fact that when we examined them we found no trace whatsoever of their having been lit in the immediate past, the wax at their tops was completely hard and cold. No candle light and certainly no music remained in the building. I walked back to my house with an uneasy mind. This time I did not search for any natural explanation and as I went down the drive I pondered Tom's description of a sound which resembled 'a couple of violins, only played much lower'. I could not help thinking of the two Wenningham cellists of the last century: the squire, whose body now rested under the Chancel, and the parson whose body had been brought back for burial just outside the little Priest's Door.

Next morning, Saturday, I told John Lester what Tom had experienced the night before. I think he had felt a little embarrassed about the events of the previous week and he was not unpleased that his story should now have received this unexpected corroboration. 'I tell you what', he said 'Something seems to have happened last night and something the Friday before: next Friday why don't you and I go and sit quietly in the church, no light or anything, and just see what happens? If there's been something odd in there the past two weeks, then it's possible something might happen again. How about it?' It is easy to be brave on a Saturday morning so I said 'Yes, certainly. I'm game. It could be interesting. Let's do that'. And so it was fixed.

The following Friday evening came. And with it, sometime after six, a telephone call from John. He was not speaking from home, he said he was speaking from near Ipswich, down at the far end of Suffolk. He had been there on business and his car had broken down. It would have to remain at the garage. He had phoned a friend in Wenningham who had very kindly agreed to go down and fetch him home. But he couldn't be back in time to keep our appointment at 8.30 pm; in fact he would not be back until ten at the earliest. Sorry. But would I go into church as we had planned, just to see whether anything would happen? As a priest, I wouldn't mind being in there on my own, would I? Not wishing to tell a downright lie, I murmured vaguely. What should I do? I certainly did not want to go alone, as I felt uneasy. But I'd got some pride left, and I was not going to admit to anyone that I, the parish priest, was afraid to go into my own parish church. Honour was at stake. But maybe, should I ring Tom, the farmer, and ask him to come along? No . . . if I did that it would be sure to get back to John and again I would look foolish. Especially if nothing happened . . .

And so just before eight-thirty I went over to church. Not exactly with alacrity, indeed I shivered and swallowed hard as I unlocked the door and I found it took quite an effort of will not to reach for the light switches as I got inside. But no, I resisted that temptation and wrapping my big priest's cloak around me, I settled down in the Churchwarden's stall at the back of the Nave to watch and wait. The moonlight, for it was a bright moonlit night, shone in through the large windows filled with clear glass, making strange pools of light on the floor and casting all kinds of hideous shadows on the whitewashed walls. The wind, as ever, sighed and moaned in the pine trees outside, and every so often there were those inexplicable creaks and rattles which are common to all old churches, but which one somehow does not seem to notice during the daytime. Now, these sounds seemed loud and threatening and at every sound and at every play of light caused by

49

the branches outside blowing in the moonlight, I felt myself freeze.

Then, suddenly and without warning I saw something quite extraordinary. Up in the Chancel, at the far end of the church, I saw the wicks of the big altar-candles glow red – just six pinpricks in the distance – glow red, and then spring into flame. They cast a light, really a surprisingly clear light, in that part of the building and although I was at some distance from them, I could see that they were burning without the slightest flicker, something most unusual when the wind is blowing outside and managing to produce considerable draughts inside. There was a pause, a pause which seemed to last a very long time but which in fact probably lasted not much more than a minute. And then, very softly at first, but gradually becoming louder and more distinct, I heard the soft, rich, sad and unmistakable sound of two cellos being played.

It is difficult, now as then, to describe my feelings. Yes, part of me was frozen with fear, but part of me wasn't. Because the sound to which I was listening, this ghostly, unearthly music was very beautiful. It was rich and mellow, mournful, yet melodious and strangely soothing. A sound which one could never forget having once heard it. And strangely, although the setting – the wind and moonlight outside the church, and the darkness and stillness within it – although these perhaps increased my fear, they also enhanced the loveliness of this phantom music. Then . . . and I regret this now . . . my fear gained the upper hand. I reached out for the bank of light switches and ran my hand roughly across them. The moonlight was shattered in an instant and replaced by the harsh light of the many electric light bulbs. In an instant the strange music-making had stopped, and as I blinked in the sudden brightness I became aware that the altar candles were once more unlit. In literally a flash, a flash of electric light, normality had returned to the church.

I was, I know, shaken. But I walked as boldly as I could up the nave and into the chancel from which the cello-playing had come. As on the previous Friday evenings, I found that everything was as normal. Except, that is, for one thing. The small Priest's Door in the South wall of the chancel, the door outside which Father Woodward lies buried and the lock of which had jammed some months before, so that I could not open it – this door now stood wide open. But as I closed the little door, securing it with its bolt, it seemed to me that I had somehow closed more than just the Priest's Door. For so far as I know, the sound of two cellos, that sad haunting sound, has not been heard again in Wenningham church.

# 7

# One Pound a Year

Like most country clergymen, I no longer live in the old rectory, but in a small modern house built within the last twenty years. One advantage of this is that I do at least live next door to the parish church, the old rectory is about half a mile away. It is a square house built in 1840, when Queen Victoria had already begun her reign. A retired couple called Harrison-West live there now and they maintain both house and garden to a standard which I could never hope to achieve. The lawns are immaculate, the flower beds filled with carefully tended bedding-out plants every Summer, whilst inside the house the furnishings and fittings are all of the best.

Soon after I came to Wenningham I called on Mr and Mrs Harrison-West. It was about four-thirty in the afternoon and they kindly offered me tea, which was served in what had been the study and was now used as a family sitting room. There was much conversation – we found that we knew some of the same people and places – and when I looked at the clock I saw that the time had got to about twenty-five minutes to six. I edged forward on my chair, waiting for my hostess to finish what she was saying before I rose and excused myself. And then, not loudly but

53

quite distinctly, there was a knock at the study door. I was taken by surprise, because already in the course of conversation they had told me that they had no resident help in the house, only two women who came in during the morning and so far as I knew no one was staying with them. There was only, I had imagined, the three of us in the Old Rectory. Oddly enough, however, neither Mr or Mrs Harrison-West seemed to take any notice of this mysterious tap on the study door. Had they not heard it? It had been perfectly audible and clear to me, and neither of them had shown any sign of deafness in the course of our conversation. I was unsure as to what I should do. I did not want to alarm them, and yet if there was someone in the house unbeknown to them, they ought to be made aware of it. So after a moment of hesitation I said 'Excuse me, but I think there was a knock at the door a moment ago'. In response to which Mr Harrison-West just glanced idly towards the door and said 'Oh yes. There often is at about this time. Don't know what it is . . . maybe something to do with the central heating. It's happened ever since we've been here. Nothing to worry about.' It was clear that they accepted this in an entirely matter of fact way, presumably through familiarity. But it seemed to be most odd to me. I found it difficult to believe that the sound was connected with the heating system and besides, it was a quite distinct tap – the sound of a finger-joint tapping against a wooden door. Furthermore, although I know very little about what people call the supernatural, I do know that animals are said to be more sensitive to unseen presences than most human beings are and on this occasion I happened to notice that the hairs on the back of Suki, the Harrison-West's little brown poodle, were bristling. I did not mention this odd experience to anyone in the village or indeed outside the village. But I did not forget it.

I suppose it was some months later that I began to take an interest in Father George Ratcliffe Woodward, the predecessor whom I mentioned in the last story. I find him a fascinating figure and I was planning to write a short memoire of him. As I began to collect material for this, I realised that I must, if at all possible, trace any of his relatives who might still be alive (he had no children) and see whether they could provide me with any reminiscences and whether they would let me examine any letters, documents, etc. which might be in their possession.

By a stroke of luck an acquaintance was able to give me the address of Father Woodward's great-nephew, Mr James Woodward, an elderly gentleman who was living at that time in Highgate, the suburb in which Father Woodward himself had spent the last twenty or thirty years of his long life. Mr Woodward was most helpful. He sent certain letters for me to copy, some notes which his great uncle had written about his childhood and education and – most important for the story which I am telling – an old notebook in which Father Woodward had kept a careful record of his expenditure during the last few years of his life. This was fascinating. It is amazing how much can be learnt about a person's interests and character by the careful study of their account book. But one item puzzled me, an item which recurred year after year. On the last day of June each year, Father Woodward had noted down 'Paid Eliza Frary of Wenningham, one pound.' Who, I wondered, could Eliza Frary have been, and why was this annual payment made to her? It was easy to answer the first question. An elderly parishioner, someone who had lived in the village all his life, was able to tell me straightaway. Eliza Frary was a village girl who had spent all her life in Wenningham, dying shortly before the Second World War. She had been, he seemed to remember, parlour maid at the rectory, but that was a very long time ago. He couldn't remember much else about her.

The second question, of why the payment of one pound a year had continued to be made annually, more than forty years after Father Woodward had left the parish, seemed much more difficult to answer. It would have been strange, I felt, for a parlour maid to be granted a 'pension for life' by someone who could not have employed her for more than six years, the length of his incumbency of Wenningham. Then again the sum of one pound, paid once a year, would seem to be a somewhat unusual kind of pension.

So when I wrote back to James Woodward, returning the various papers he had lent me and thanking him for allowing me to see and copy them, I drew his attention to this particular item in his great-uncle's account book. And I explained that since it referred to the maintenance of a link with Wenningham nearly half a century after he had been incumbent, it was naturally something which interested me. Mr Woodward answered my letter almost by return of post. It so happened, he wrote, that he could indeed explain the recurring entry about which I had inquired and he thought that the story behind it might interest me. It was, he said, a story which his uncle had told him on a number of occasions when he was a boy, and it had stuck in his memory.

It was important to remember, he wrote, that priests of his great-uncle's generation tended to be very regular in their habits, and perhaps none more so than those who had come under the influence of the Oxford Movement, as Father Woodward had done, with its emphasis upon self-discipline and pastoral zeal. It had been his rule, apparently, to visit in the parish each afternoon between two and four-thirty. At four-thirty he would return to the rectory for tea and then, in view of the fact that he had risen at six in the morning, he would allow himself a short rest. But his parlour maid, at least during the first three years of his time in Wenningham, had strict instructions to knock on the door of his study at precisely five-thirty. Then, if he had been dozing, he would wake up and set off for church, allowing himself ten to fifteen minutes for private prayer before Evensong, which was sung at six.

One day, however, a day in June 1885, Eliza Frary his parlour maid quite simply forgot to knock on the study door at five-thirty. Presumably she had been engrossed in some job in the house and this particular task had slipped her mind. When she noticed the clock it said five thirty-five. She hurried to the study, knocked and found that the Rector had indeed been asleep. She apologized for being five minutes late, was told not to worry as there was still plenty of time to get to church for Evensong, and that seemed to be that.

As the rector set out the sky was already very dark, made so by an approaching storm. Probably it was one of those memorable occasions when the last rays of sunshine cast a brilliant light upon the trees before the storm breaks, making them stand out vividly against the deep grey sky. Soon the first rumbles of thunder were heard in the distance, the storm was coming nearer. Then, as now, the lane leading from the old rectory towards the church was lined with tall trees, beeches, oaks, sykamores and the final stretch before the church is reached is fairly straight. As Father Woodward came to this part of the road there was a blinding flash of lightening and with an ear-splitting crackle followed by a violent rending tearing sound, one of the larger oak trees at the far end of that piece of road was struck and torn from top to bottom. The Rector, his great-nephew remembered, had understandably been shaken by this event. But not only shaken, he had been decidedly effected by it. With perhaps just a hint of that Victorian love of the melodramatic, he had always in future referred to 'the day of his deliverance', for had he been a few hundred yards further along the road he would, he maintained, certainly have been killed. And his deliverance was due, he believed, entirely to Eliza Frary who had woken him up five minutes later than usual. For had she woken him at the normal time of five-thirty, he had repeated, then he would almost certainly have been either under, or very close to, the oak at the moment when the lightening struck it.

So, Mr Woodward concluded, his great-uncle had promised to give Eliza Frary one pound each year on the anniversary of that June day, as an act of gratitude for the (highly unusual) way in which she had saved his life. And this he continued to do, right up to the time of his death in Highgate nearly half a century later. He also, James Woodward added, gave strict instructions to Eliza that in future she must never again knock at the study door at five-thirty but must be careful to knock at precisely five-thirtyfive, as she had so fortunately done on that afternoon in June 1885.

It seems, I thought as I read the letter, that she still does so.

# 8

# The Priory Lake

Mention has already been made of the big house in Wenningham, called The Priory because it is built on the site of the mediaeval priory which once dominated the village, and also of the Calthorpe family, who lived in the house for nearly three centuries. Now when the last Calthorpe squire died unmarried in 1916, it was not the first time that the family had become extinct in the male line. Just over a century before, in 1804, another bachelor squire had died and with him had ended the original line of Calthorpes. At his death the estate had passed to a distant cousin, a clergyman, who took the name and arms of Calthorpe and as Daniel Henry Calthorpe proceeded to take up residence at Wenningham. Very soon he – or more probably his wife – found the old priory house (which is, in fact, the mediaeval Prior's Lodging, remodelled in the early years of the eighteenth century) inconvenient and old-fashioned. He was now a man of considerable means and also the father of an increasing family. So he set about extending and improving the old house, installing new windows, doorcases and fireplaces, and incorporating a fine new staircase surmounted by an elaborate lantern. Once the house had been brought up to date,

Daniel Calthorpe then turned his attention to the grounds. Mid-eighteenth century prints show a layout of carefully trimmed yew hedges – a style of gardening which had become unfashionable at least half a century before his succession. These the new squire swept away, replacing them with the kind of landscape garden which in most places had been laid out some decades earlier. His scheme of 1806 must have been one of the very last eighteenth century-type landscapes to have been created on a Norfolk estate.

No landscape of the kind which Daniel Henry Calthorpe wished to lay out was considered complete unless it included a lake. It so happened that the lie of the land around the Priory made the creation of an ornamental lake difficult. The village lay to one side of the house, the main Norwich road on another, whilst on a third stands the fairly large parish church. The fourth side was, as it happened, the main front of the house, but on this side a small river ran just a couple of hundred yards from the front door and beyond that the land begins to rise quite sharply. A lake, however, there had to be and so the little River Stewkey was duly dammed and sluiced and thereby swollen into a lake. It could not be a large lake, the site demanded that it must be long and somewhat narrow and its proximity to the house was unusual, but there had been little choice regarding size and position. It had to be there or nowhere. Early nineteenth century prints and later nineteenth century photographs however, show the scheme to have been not unsuccessful. The house, being so near the lake, was reflected in it in a very pleasing way and trees had been planted to overhang its waters at one end, at the other a picturesque bridge had been built. One gets the impression that the family took rather a pride in the lake, for the later photographs show that a boathouse had been built on one side, despite the fact that the limited extent of the water hardly made it suitable for boating. Be that as it may, the fact is that the priory lake no longer exists and only some-one who had seen the old prints and photographs would ever suppose that it had been. It is possible I found, to pick out the area which it once covered and maybe the grass within those boundaries is a little greener and a little longer than the grass in the park-land beyond. But the River Stewkey, which is really little more than a stream and which wanders so casually across the site of the former lake, is far from inclined to suggest the sheet of ornamental water in which Wenningham Priory once found itself reflected.

But when did the priory lake disappear, and why? Lakes on country estates, even artificial lakes, do not come and go overnight. Normally care is taken over their creation and so long as the estate is still func-tioning a reasonable amount of care is taken over their maintenance. Once I knew that there had been a lake in the priory grounds, having seen the prints and photographs which depicted it, I became intrigued as to why it had been allowed to vanish. I thought that I had found the answer when I learned about the 1912 flood. Details of how that flood had been caused, whether by a sudden thaw of snow in Winter or by torrential storm-rains in Summer, were difficult to come by. But photographs of the flood itself were still in circulation, showing the village street under a foot or two of water, with rowing-boats (heaven knows where from) carrying supplies to marooned parishioners who hung out from their bedroom windows! And I heard a story too, about the last eccentric Calthorpe squire and the flood: of how he insisted on dining in his dining room downstairs at the priory, even though the carpet was rising and falling upon several inches of water and was adamant in refusing his butler's suggestion that he should move upstairs!

So I put two and two together, as I thought, and decided that it must obviously have been the waters of the 1912 flood which had brought the priory lake to an end. The flood waters bearing down along the course of the river – which, you will remember, ran through the lake – and sweeping away the dam and the sluice which held the lake in place. From there, it was easy to presume that the old and eccentric squire, who in 1912 was within four years of his death, had simply never bothered to have the dam rebuilt and the lake restored. That was what I supposed. But one Winter's afternoon, sitting in the twilight with an elderly parishioner, I learned a very different and even more dramatic story of how the lake came to an end. In the course of which I discovered two things: first, that its demise was no accident brought about by floodwater and second, that the lake had ceased to exist a couple of years before the great flood of 1912.

I had heard before that the last Calthorpe squire had an odd affection for children and indeed I have mentioned the fact in another story. You may remember how he used to throw boiled sweets over the wall surrounding his grounds to be caught by children who happened to pass that way on their way to Catechism. Apparently the children were somewhat frightened of him. He must have presented an odd appearance with his Tam O'Shanter hat and his shoes often one brown and one black and after all, he was the squire – still a person to be reckoned with in the England of pre-First World War days. Nevertheless, the elderly lady with whom I was sitting told me his benefactions to the village children were not limited to boiled sweets. There were other occasions when he 'made a gesture' as she rather quaintly put it and one of these occasions was when (and it seemed an annual event in those far-off days) the priory lake was frozen over in Winter. It would be announced in the village school that Mr Calthorpe had invited the children to skate or slide on his lake (many children, of course, did not possess skates) and then on the following Saturday, or indeed after school if it was a clear night, large numbers of the village children would make their way down to the lake and have great fun skating or sliding. Mr Calthorpe himself, being a shy man, did not appear. On these merry occasions he watched the children not from behind his wall, but from an upstairs window of the priory, which of course commanded a complete view of the fun and games taking place on the lake immediately in front of the house.

It was the first day of the skating and sliding some-time in January 1910, the old lady told me and the usual announcement had been made at the beginning of afternoon school. Excitement had mounted and as soon as lessons ended a noisy and enthusiastic crowd of children made their way down the priory drive, those with skates running home first to fetch them and those without making their way to the frozen lake without delay. Being January, dusk followed by darkness came quickly, but the sky had been clear all day and soon a full moon was mounting in the cloud-less sky. So the coming of nightfall put no immediate end to the sports. Gradually, however, tea time came and as they became wet as well as hungry the chil-dren started to drift home. After a while only a few of them were left on the lake, and then finally just one, Simon, son of the head woodman on the estate. He was a shy solitary boy, in some ways perhaps not unlike the old squire himself. He also had undoubted skill as a skater. Up and down the lake he sped, to and fro, circling elegantly and effortlessly in the bright moonlight watched by an engrossed Henry James Calthorpe from his unlit upstairs window.

As the old lady told me her tale the dusk gathered, just as it had done on that January day so many years before. And as her tale unfolded I could foresee its conclusion. Somewhere in the middle of the lake the ice cracked and gave way. This was the first day of skating, the first day when it had been thought suffi-ciently hard to permit the sport. The decision had been wrong. Maybe the large number of children which had been on the ice had weakened it. Be that as it may, it suddenly cracked and the boy screamed as it gave way beneath him. The squire, who had seen and heard all, rushed downstairs across the pillared-entrance hall of his house, out of the front door and down to the lake, shouting, crying-out, and knowing in his heart all the time that it was too late, that nothing could be done.

After that terrible accident Mr Calthorpe was never the same, the old lady continued. He became more withdrawn, almost a recluse until he died a few years later. But the very day after that awful tragedy, a tragedy which he had witnessed and had been powerless to prevent – and one, moreover, for which he felt directly responsible because he had invited the children to the lake – he ordered the dam and sluice to be dismantled and the lake drained. The estate men worked with pick axes, trying to move the frozen bricks and stones, until eventually the lower, un-frozen, waters of the lake gushed out and away down the course of the river, leaving the frozen upper-water of the lake lying on its floor like the broken pieces of some huge mirror. After some days the ice had melted leaving only the mud which, before many months were passed, had begun to green over. And so in the saddest and most unforeseen cir-cumstances, the priory lake came to an end, just over one hundred years after its enthusiastic creation.

But the old lady's story did not end there. Lower-ing her voice as she poked the fire, now with the growing darkness the only source of light in the room, she confided something further. Namely, that she had known people down the years who, when walking down the drive to the Priory on a Winters night, but only, she added, when there was a sharp frost and a full moon, had heard the screams of the boy and the cries of the old man. And that those who had heard those sounds had never forgotten them. They were sounds, she said, so horrible and so haunting that those who heard them would take their memory with them to the grave.

# 9

# The Penitent

There is a notice in the porch of Wenningham church which reads 'The Rector is available to hear Confessions most evenings at 7.15 pm, and at any other time by appointment'. And so he is. Each day Evensong is said at seven o'clock in St Anne's Chapel, which lies on the North side of the chancel and when it ends I get up from my stall and look down into the nave to see whether or not anyone is waiting. Except before major festivals there usually isn't anyone, but when there is, they invariably kneel in one of the pews in the South aisle as they wait, because the confessional is placed in St Catherine's Chapel, the side chapel which lies to the South of the chancel, balancing that on the north.

The incident I want to relate took place about five years ago, in early November. By seven-fifteen it was quite dark. As usual a light was on at the back of church and of course the lights were on in St Anne's Chapel for Evensong, but the rest of the church was in darkness. The service having ended, I got up and glanced down into the nave. There, in the deep shadows of the South aisle, I could see that there was in fact someone kneeling down, someone who was presumably waiting to make their confession. So

I went into the sacristy and put on the customary cotta and purple stole; I crossed the chancel, turned on the lights in St. Catherine's Chapel and knelt before the altar to say a prayer. Then I went over to the confessional, which stands in one corner of the chapel and sat down. Maybe I should explain that our confessional is not the kind of 'box' which one finds in many Roman Catholic churches, just a chair for the priest and a prayer-desk for the penitent, with a simple oak screen between them pierced by a lattice-work grille.

After a few moments I heard footsteps advancing along the aisle and up the three or four steps which lead up into the chapel. As the penitent came into the light I recognised her straight away; an elderly lady from the parish, someone whom I had visited on two or three occasions but whom I could not remember ever having seen in church before. I was somewhat taken aback therefore that she should now present herself in the confessional. I remembered that she had once told me that she used to go to church when she was a girl, that she had been confirmed and I remembered vaguely that she had mentioned making her confession when she was young, maybe sixty-odd years ago. But she had not, so far as I knew, done anything about the practice of the faith for many years, certainly not during my time in Wenningham. Be that as it may, a priest is trained never to express surprise in the confessional and I knew by experience that it is far from unknown for someone to come to this sacrament quite unexpectedly, especially when under stress.

The old lady knelt down and I began to give her the customary blessing which precedes the actual confession of sin: 'The Lord be in your heart and on your lips, that you may have grace to make a true confession of all your sins, in the Name of the Father and of the Son and of the Holy Spirit, Amen.' In those few seconds I became aware that she was in some distress. Choking back her tears, she began, very hesitantly, to read the words printed on the card before her, words which once, long ago, had probably been familiar, but which now required careful reading. 'I confess to Almight God . . . the Father, the Son, . . . and the Holy Spirit . . . and to you, Father, . . . that I have sinned very much in thought . . . word, and deed, . . . by my own fault . . .'. It took quite a while (I suppose in reality not more than a couple of minutes, but it seemed a long time) for her to get through this first part of the confession. And then, after a further pause, she launched into her story. Very haltingly at first and then with growing confidence. Since I am not naming the penitent and because I think it would be impossible for you to identify her, I intend to set down the bare bones of what she said; indeed I must do so if you are to understand what followed.

It seemed that many years before when she was a girl in her late teens, the old lady had been in service at one of the big houses in the area (again, I must not name the house). Her father, it seemed, had been a very unsavoury character, guilty of a certain amount of cruelty to his wife and children and feared by them all. She had been the eldest child and consequently

73

the first to leave home. Once a week she was given an afternoon off and she used it to walk the five miles or so home in order to see her family. On those occasions she had talked, quite naturally, about the house where she worked and about all the beautiful things it contained – the pictures, furniture, silver, tapestries and about the lovely clothes and jewellery worn by the women of the house. Her father had latched on to this and before long he had begun to try to persuade her to steal a piece of jewellery. At first she had been very distressed by this suggestion. She had cried and said that she wouldn't consider doing such a dreadful thing. But week by week he had pressed her to bring something home – a bracelet, a ring, maybe some diamond ear-rings – something, he said, which he could sell to provide extra comfort for the family. She would never be caught he urged, if she was careful. She could hide the piece of jewellery and then get it home, maybe in her clothes and no one would be able to prove anything. For months she resisted these suggestions, these requests, which became more and more insistent. And then in the Winter her mother became ill. Not surprisingly her father used this to increase the pressure on his daughter. He said how much her mother needed medicine, special food, more fuel. He told her how heartless she was not to provide her mother with the means to these things when it would be so very easy for her to do so. He said she was selfish and that the ladies at the House could well afford to lose just one piece of their jewellery; it wouldn't make them sick and cold and hungry, as her mother was, would it?

She had only been a teenager at the time and understandably this pressure, this emotional blackmail, had become too much for her. It so happened that a large house party was about to take place, a number of wealthy women would be staying and it would not be unusual for pieces of jewellery to be left about on dressing-tables. . . . So she did as her father had requested, indeed insisted. She took a diamond and emerald ring belonging to a titled lady whom she still remembered came from Northamptonshire. Before long the ring was missed, but not before it had been sewn into the hem of her skirt. There was a great hew and cry, for apparently the ring was of considerable value and in the servants hall there was much rumour and speculation. Suspicion fell on another young maid called Molly because she had been seen near to the room from which the ring had been taken (doubtless about her normal business) shortly before it had been missed. She protested her innocence in vain: she was accused, disgraced and dismissed without a reference, even though there was no firm evidence against her. My penitent had wanted to own up, but had been too afraid. And so the ring was passed to her father who sold it in a local town for a fraction of its true value and of the money he received for it, very little indeed was used for the benefit of his sick wife.

Well this was the substance of what the old lady had come to confess to God. The telling of it took some time, for understandably it was not told in the concise and coherent way in which I have tried to set it down. She was very distressed and in a highly emotional state. Feelings of guilt and fear which had festered inside her for more than half-a-century were at last finding expression and being brought to the surface. On the one hand she found it extremely difficult to make her confession and yet on the other, she longed for the relief which only the telling of her story to another person could bring. At last she had finished and she stammered out the final words of the form of confession. 'For these and for all my other sins which I cannot now remember, I am heartily sorry, firmly intend to amend, humbly ask pardon of God, and of you, Father, advice, penance and absolution.' Then it was my turn to speak and I gave her, I hope, words of comfort, reassurance and encouragement, for I knew that these were the things which she needed. I tried to impress upon her the fact of the love and understanding of God and to remind her that her theft, wrong though it had been, had not been motivated by any wish for personal gain but by the wholly good desire to bring comfort to her sick mother. As a result of having unburdened her conscience and of having received the gift of absolution and maybe too, as a result of having taken to heart the words that I had been led to use in giving her counsel, she became calm. She had, I felt, accepted the fact that God had answered her very deep and sincere penitence with forgiveness. She left the confessional, I believe, with something of the peace and comfort and confidence which is so often experienced by those who use this sacrament.

When she had gone down the steps leading back into the South aisle I rose from my seat, prayed again for a moment before the altar and then crossed the chancel again to the sacristy, where I took off my cotta and stole. I had not heard the sound of the somewhat noisy church door being opened and closed and so I supposed that my penitent was still praying in the darkened nave. I hung around for a while. I did a few jobs in the sacristy, I put out the lamps burning before one or two of the statues. And then I felt that it was really time to lock the church for the night and go home. So I went into the nave but I could not see the woman, I put on the lights, but there was no sign of her. Well, I thought, how very quietly she must have left the church: I certainly had not heard the sound of the door. But then, I reflected, how quietly she must have come in during Evensong too; for it had not been until I looked down the nave after the Office that I'd known she was there . . .

The interview in the confessional had taken quite a while and it was well after eight o'clock as I walked down the drive to the rectory. The telephone was ringing. I ran the last few yards, fumbled with my keys, opened the front door and went into the study expecting that the phone would stop ringing just as I reached it, as so often happens. I picked up the receiver and said 'Wenningham Rectory'. It was our local undertaker, Mr Canford. He had rung, he said, to tell me that one of my parishioners had died and to arrange a funeral. As always when I receive these calls I asked anxiously and apprehensively who it was, afraid that it might be someone I knew well. But I was taken aback, indeed made incredulous, when the undertaker said the name of the woman whose confession I had just heard. Oh no, I said immediately, you have got the wrong name. As it happens I've just seen so-and-so, so it can't possibly be her. (I did not, of course, divulge where I had seen her or for what purpose). But the undertaker persisted, giving the address which was certainly the address of the woman I had just been with in church. Then something occurred to me. Perhaps it was her daughter-in-law who had died? The surname was the same, and I knew that mother, son and daughter-in-law all shared a house and so had the same address. No, the undertaker insisted, it was the old lady. He knew perfectly well who it was, he said a little crossly. In fact he had just removed the body to his Chapel of Rest, so there could really be no doubt. I must have seen someone else, he said, someone like the deceased. Well when had she died? I questioned, utterly perplexed. Mid-afternoon, came the reply. She had had a heart-attack he informed me and had died shortly afterwards.

We fixed a day and a time for the funeral and the undertaker rang off. It was quite beyond me, I could make no sense of it. Normally in the case of a bereavement in a non-church family I probably would not feel the need to make a visit immediately, especially in the mid-to-late evening. I would visit the following day. But this case was so extraordinary that even though it was now after eight-thirty I decided to go round to the house straight away. My mind was in a turmoil as I got out of the car and walked up the path. I did not know quite what to say. The undertaker had solemnly assured me that the woman had been dead since mid-afternoon and yet I knew full well that I had been hearing her confession less than an hour ago. As I rang the doorbell it was obvious that I would have to play this one by ear, trying to gauge the true situation by what I found.

The door was opened by the daughter-in-law, so I knew straight away that it wasn't her who had died. Her eyes were red and there was that whole atmosphere of bereavement, confirmed most obviously by the fact that she stood back for me to enter, something which always happens when one visits the bereaved. For once, the priest is expected to call and to come in. The people he is visiting know precisely why he is there and there isn't the hesitation and uncertainty which so often greets the priest in his general visiting.

She paused in the narrow hall of the council house, her hand on the door handle of the living-room and said in a low confidential voice 'I'm glad you've come, Father . . . you heard about Alf's mother . . . it was very sudden, about half-past-three. He was in, we both were, and he's taken it very badly. She had the attack and then we had a terrible ten minutes with her before she died . . . she was in a lot of pain and in a right state too, trying to say something and not able to get it out. Anyway, come and see him . . .'.

We went into the living room. Her husband was sitting on the settee, his head between his hands. 'Alf' the woman said 'here's Father come to see you. Come on now, he wants to talk to you'. (This is always, I find, assumed to be the case – that the priest visiting the bereaved has come to say something!) The man only shook his head, still between his hands, and did not look up. So his wife continued, perceptively, 'Now you tell him what happened, Alf. It might help you to tell Father about it . . . I'll go and make a cup of tea'.

When she had left the room I said how sorry I had been to hear of his mother's death. I said I gathered that it had been sudden, had she been ill recently? Had they known that she had heart trouble? Then gradually he began to give me a detailed account, as mourners often wish to do, of what had happened that afternoon. 'But Father', he said, coming to the matter for which his wife had sought to prepare me, 'what upset us more than anything else was that she was so upset, in such a state, those last ten minutes. Trying to tell us something. I suppose it was something she'd got on her mind, something that was worrying her. But she just couldn't say what she wanted to. She'd got nothing that I know to worry about; she was a good-living woman, never spoke a wrong word of anyone. Something about a ring, we could make that out. And about someone called Molly. I don't know of anyone called Molly and I don't know that she did. I'd never heard her mention anyone by that name. But such a state she was in and there was nothing we could do. It's awful thinking of her dying with something worrying her so much . . .'

It seemed that I now had to comfort and reassure the son just as earlier that evening I had tried to comfort and reassure the mother; yes, for I was absolutely certain about what had taken place in church and especially so after what the man had told me. What can one best say to a bereaved person? It is never easy to know what to say, but in this case it was quite clear. Sitting down beside the man I told him slowly and gently that Christians believe that after death it is possible for us to find a real and lasting peace for our minds and hearts, a peace which cannot always be achieved in this life. A freedom from anxiety which is born from the forgiveness which God wants to give us and which it is never too late for us to ask for. As I talked to him about this, I seemed to hear again in my mind the quavering, hesitant voice of the old lady 'I confess to Almighty God, the Father, the Son and the Holy Spirit, that I have sinned very much in thought and word and deed . . . for these and for all my other sins which I cannot now remember, I am heartily sorry, and humbly ask pardon of God . . .'. And what I said to the man about the forgiveness of God and the peace of mind which it brings to us, I said with a depth of conviction which I had never experienced before, and maybe, I fear, will never know in quite the same way again.

# 10

# A Complimentary Lunch

North Norfolk is a popular place for retirement and a number of retired people live in Wenningham. Among them is a priest, Canon Parker, who was formerly Vicar of a large parish in South London. Rene, his wife, is an accomplished cook and they are very hospitable and so I am quite often invited to have supper with them. As I live alone and cook (theoretically) for myself, such invitations are most welcome and an evening spent with the Parkers is always something to look forward to.

Last Autumn the Canon and his wife had been away for a week staying with their son who is in practice as a general practitioner in Essex. On their return they phoned and asked whether I would like to join them for supper on the following Sunday evening and I was delighted to say yes. And so it was that a day or two later I found myself in their comfortable sitting room, warming my feet by a log fire and drinking sherry with the Canon whilst Rene finished off the preparations for the meal in the kitchen.

In the course of conversation I asked how they had got on in Essex. Had the family been well? Had there been any outings? And how had the journey gone. It is quite a long drive from North Norfolk down to the Essex coast? 'Yes', he said, 'it is quite a distance but we take our time over it. One of the joys of being retired is not having to rush. And we always make a point of stopping on the way and having a really good lunch. We usually manage to find a decent restaurant and we give ourselves a treat. A stop for lunch, maybe for a couple of hours, breaks up the journey very well.' I went on to ask him where they had stopped this time, because I too like eating out and it is always useful to know about a good place. It was this question of mine which prompted him to tell me the following story.

'Well,' he began, 'we stopped in a small town in Suffolk' – he mentioned the name – 'it was about twelve-thirty and we thought that we could probably find somewhere there. Do you know it? – a charming old place. The main street is full of old houses quite a number of them half-timbered and others with that pink-washed plasterwork that you get such a lot in Suffolk. Half way down the street we found a restaurant called The Old Bakery. Rather a nice building, built of mellow red bricks, and dating I should think from the early eighteenth century. When we got in we could see that it had indeed been a bakery; they'd kept the old ovens in the room at the back and in the front, which is the main part of the restaurant, they'd kept the old counter where the bread used to be sold. The menu was very good and not at all expensive for these days. They'd got some unusual things on it, like the dish we had for a first-course, spiced peaches: peaches filled with a mixture of cream cheese and spices and then put under the grill with grated cheese on top. Delicious. In fact I think Rene is going to try it out for a first course this evening. And then afterwards we had chicken pancakes – savoury pancakes filled with pieces of chicken, and then with a sauce made from wine and cream poured over it. Well anyway, it was very good, and when we left we said we would try to call there again on the way home; once you find a place that's really good you're quite keen to go back!

It so happened – well really I'd planned it quite carefully – that coming back we arrived in the same market town at about the same time. It was last Thursday and again we had another excellent meal at The Old Bakery. I won't tell you what we had the second time, or else you might feel too full for your supper which should be ready in a few minutes. Anyhow, when we'd finished I asked the waitress for the bill. 'Oh, I don't think Mrs whatever-her-name-was, the wife of the owner-chef, I don't think she's going to let you pay'. Well we thought that sounded rather extraordinary. The week before we'd certainly told her how much we'd enjoyed the cooking and I expect they were pleased to see customers back again, but it still seemed pretty strange for them to want to give us this second meal free of charge. So I said to the waitress that I'd like to have a word with Mrs whatever-her-name-was and she said she would fetch her. A couple of minutes later she appeared. Yes, it was quite correct, she said, there was no charge. It was to be on the house. We said that this was very kind, but we couldn't possibly not pay . . . she was in business and besides, whatever made her want to be so generous to us? (admittedly I was dressed as a clergyman, but I didn't think we looked as hard up as all that!) 'Well,' she said with a smile, 'it is for services rendered – yes, it is because I want to show my gratitude for something which you did when you were here last week.' What? I asked in astonishment. I couldn't think of anything I had done to be of service. All I had done was to sit down to an excellent lunch. In reply, she said that she would tell us what it was. Yes, she would like us to know. Then we would see exactly why it was that she wanted us to have a complimentary lunch. She drew up a chair, and in a quiet voice, because there were other people eating at other tables, she told us this rather surprising story.

She and her husband had bought The Old Bakery about four years ago. They had bought it from the people who had converted it from a bakery to a restaurant a few years previously. One of the things which had attracted them to it, she said, was that from the very first time they had gone to look at it, they had been aware of the place having a good feeling, a very good atmosphere. She was, she said, very sensitive to places and their atmosphere: she felt that this was a place where people had been at peace, at peace with life and with themselves. And when they had moved in and begun life at The Old Bakery she'd been even more aware of this and of something very strange but very nice – namely the fact that although it was by then well over ten years since the place had actually functioned as a bakery there seemed to be –

particularly in the morning – a distinct smell of newly-baked bread. No, it wasn't just her who was aware of this, her husband and their two children had all been aware of this particular smell from time to time. And if this was some kind of haunting, well, what a nice kind of haunting to have! – newly-baked bread, one of the nicest smells imaginable.

But then about a year ago, she told us, something quite inexplicable happened. The smell of newly-baked bread had suddenly vanished, and in its place had come a strange, unpleasant smell. It was difficult to describe, not at all distinct as the other one had been. Just a bad sort of smell, a smell of mustiness and decay. Again, all of them had smelt it on and off and also, the family had gradually become aware of a change in atmosphere. The good, pleasant, cheerful atmosphere seemed somehow to have gone. They had no idea why this change had come about; they couldn't put their finger on any kind of alteration in their relationships or in the building itself which might have triggered it off. They found the smell and the atmosphere which seemed to go with it, very difficult to live with. They'd tried all kinds of things but nothing seemed to drive it away. And sometimes it was present in the restaurant, which was hardly good for custom. In fact they were aware that they had been losing trade in the past few months, and they felt quite sure that this bad smell which they could not explain or irradicate was the cause of it.

'Well,' she continued, 'you came here last week, and the very next morning, last Friday, we got up and came down and what did we smell? – that good smell of newly-baked bread back again! You can't think what a joy and a relief it was to us. Especially as that heavy atmosphere seemed to have somehow gone as well. And since then, we've smelt the bread a number of times, and never once has any of us come across the other smell. As you can imagine, we started asking ourselves what it could possibly be that had brought the change about – what, or who, could have driven that bad smell and bad atmosphere away? We puzzled over it for a day or two. And then I said to my husband, I've got it. Last Thursday lunch time there was a priest here, a priest and his wife. And before they had their meal, he prayed and made the sign of the Cross'. Prayed? I asked in surprise. 'Yes', she said – 'you said grace before you began your first-course. I happened to notice'. 'Oh yes', I replied, slightly embarrassed, 'we do always say grace at home and I suppose by force of habit – that rather than piety – I do often find myself saying it when we're eating in a restaurant.' 'Well,' she continued, 'I felt absolutely certain when I remembered what you had done that it must be because a priest had prayed in the house that the bad smell, whatever it was, had gone. I could think of nothing else, no other reason for its going. We felt so grateful to you. And I said to my husband, if they do call back again, as they said they might do, then we must give them a complimentary lunch.'

As the Canon came to the end of the story, the sitting room door opened and Rene told us that supper was now of the table. We followed her across the hall and into the dining room and we did indeed start with the spiced peaches, which were delicious. As usual the Canon said grace and I was interested to note that the grace which he used had been slightly amended: to the request that we might be given thankful hearts was added the request (echoing the words of the Lord's Prayer) that we might be delivered from all evil. Which addition, in view of the apparent power of the ordinary form of the grace, I thought hardly necessary . . .!

# 11

# The Priest's Door

Harton St George is about a mile and a half from Wenningham and with a population of under fifty people it is a hamlet rather than a village. Before the last war, when agriculture was still unmechanized and many more people were employed on the land, at least twice as many people lived at Harton. In those days it had its own public house, The Buck, and there was a resident priest, a curate-in-charge appointed by the Rector of Wenningham, living in the old Parsonage which stands behind the church. But since the war the Parsonage has been sold as a private house and there is now only one service each week at the church, a Eucharist at ten o'clock each Sunday morning.

St George' Church, the East wall of which almost juts out into the road running through Harton, is very small by Norfolk standards, which suggests that Harton itself was never a thriving or populous settlement. The church has a simple tower with neither buttresses nor battlements, capped by a low lead-covered pyramid-roof, a long narrow nave and chancel with no structural division between them and no aisles, and a small one-storey South porch. Inside there is a fine chancel screen dating from the early years of the sixteenth century, its panels painted with female saints and the doctors of the church. Besides the screen, which divides the nave from the chancel, the only other item of special interest is the set of fifteenth century poppy-head bench ends.

By the mid 1870s the church was apparently in a bad state of repair. A contemporary description speaks of it as being 'in a ruinous and most unsafe state and totally unfit for the purpose of divine worship'. Some ten or fifteen years before this description was written, the squire, Henry Calthorpe, had caused Wenningham church to undergo an extensive restoration and now he turned his attention to Harton. At Wenningham he had employed the celebrated Victorian architect George Edmund Street. For Harton he chose another leading architect of the period, W. Eden Nesfield. It so happens that Nesfield's specification for the work and a number of his drawings survive in the Calthorpe Papers at the Norfolk Records Office in Norwich and these are of considerable interest. Just a few years earlier architects engaged upon the restoration of churches – and an extraordinary number of parish churches underwent restoration in the middle years of the last century – tended to take considerable liberties. Often they would sweep away genuine mediaeval features and furnishings, replacing them with new work of their own design. But then, as the century advanced, a new approach to church restoration developed, one which was altogether more sensitive and sympathetic, with the architect seeking to conserve the old work rather than to renew or replace it. Nesfield was one of the leaders in this new approach, and his specification for the rebuilding of Harton church (for it was found to be nothing less than a rebuilding from the foundations which was required) making interesting and heartening reading. He informed the contractor that

> 'the whole of the walls are to be re-built with rubble of the same thickness as the present ones and on the old foundations and in exactly similar character to the old walls. The old facing stones, quoins, windows, jambs and heads internally and externally and rubble work are to be re-used so far as they are sound and approved by the architect, great care being taken to place each stone so re-used in exactly the same position that it previously occupied.'

Now when I read Nesfield's specification in the Records Office there was one detail about it which puzzled me because it seemed to be quite out of character with all the rest. It was the single bald statement that 'the old doorway in the South wall of the chancel will not be re-built'. I knew from old prints of the church and from some rather hazy photographs in our Parish Records (taken in 1879, just before the re-building was begun) that there certainly had been a small doorway on the South side of the chancel. Most mediaeval churches have such a doorway and it is usually called the Priest's Door. I also knew that no such doorway exists in Harton church as it was rebuilt under Nesfield's direction. Reading his specification, which made his conservative attitude towards the restoration so clear, I found it quite incomprehensible that whilst every other detail of the ancient building had to be replaced, or exactly reproduced if the stone was no longer good, yet such an important feature as a doorway should simply be omitted. If, for some reason to do with draughts or the re-arrangement of the seating, the old Priest's Door was undesirable, then surely one would have expected that at least the stonework would have been incorporated into the re-built wall, with the opening simply built up with flints. But no, there was to be no trace whatsoever of the former doorway. And no explanation given, only the simple statement in the specification 'the old doorway in the South side of the present chancel will not be re-built'.

Then in 1978, the General Synod of the Church of England made a ruling that all church records over one hundred years old must be deposited in the appropriate Diocesan Records Office unless the parish concerned could ensure that they would be kept under controlled atmospheric conditions. With constant demands to pay for restoration work on our churches the purchase of whatever equipment would be necessary to create such conditions could not seriously be considered. Consequently the Parochial Church Council decided that we should deposit our records at Norwich and I began the task of gathering together and sorting out our registers, books and documents ready for them to be collected by the Diocesan Archivist. It was surprising just how much material there was, and how varied. The actual registers had been kept in a safe in the sacristy of the Parish church, but the rest of the material had been stored partly at the vicarage – under the stairs, in unused wardrobes and on my study shelves – and partly in three wooden trunks in the ringing chamber of the tower at Wenningham.

The most interesting part of the process proved to be sorting out the contents of those three trunks. To my shame I had never looked through these before and not surprisingly they yielded up some items of real interest. There was a set of nineteenth century service registers, there was music used by the church choir a hundred years ago; there was a series of minute books recording the meetings of the governors of the former church school: together, these gave fascinating insights into the life of the Parish as it was lived a century ago. There was also items which related specifically to Harton St George. I found, for example, items as varied as the bills for cleaning materials purchased for the church in the 1920s, and the faculty document authorising the rebuilding in 1879. But most interesting of all was a book labelled on its spine *The Harton St George Church Log Book*. I found that this had been begun and very faithfully kept by the curate-in-charge at Harton from 1877 to 1885, a period which of course covered the rebuilding of the church. There was an entry, sometimes very brief and sometimes more extended, for almost every day during that eight-year period and these entries recorded all kinds of parish, local and even national events. It was, I recognised straightaway, a most valuable and important record of life as it had been lived in a small Norfolk village in the last century.

As I read through the log book, I was fascinated by the account it gave of the rebuilding of Harton church. Day by day the writer noted down the progress of the work, from the dismantling of the fabric right through to the completion of the reconstruction. He had written down precisely what work was done on each particular day. But it was the entry from September 7th 1879 which caught my attention. For there I found written:

'Today the men began to rebuild the South wall of the chancel. Mr Nesfield has instructed them to omit the Priest's Door. I trust that this will be the end of the inconvenience I have suffered'.

After these words he had placed an asterisk, directing the reader to the bottom of the page, where he had added in his small neat handwriting the following words of explanation:

'The inconvenience I refer to is this. When I am engaged upon saying the daily offices, the door in the South wall is wont to open, seemingly of its own accord, and the sound of feet is heard as if entering the chancel. Nothing is seen. I take this to be one of my predecessors in the cure of souls here, most likely from some century past, who in spirit enters to join me at my prayers. This ghostly entrance has been both inconvenient to me and alarming to any people who may have come to say the office with me. Therefore I have insisted, with Mr Calthorpe's entire agreement, that the door should not be replaced, which I trust will put an end to this strange and unwelcome intrusion'.

Ah, I thought, so this explains the seeming incongruity in Nesfield's specification, the careful preservation and re-instatement of everything except the Priest's Door. How extraordinary. And how ingenious on the part of the curate-in-charge! For whilst I do not ever say the daily offices at Harton, saying them in the church at Wenningham, which almost adjoins my house, I have, nevertheless, never heard anyone speak of a ghostly entry into Harton church. It appeared that the blocking up, or rather total omission of the doorway, together with the complete reconstruction of the church itself, had served to lay once and for all this harmless but inconvenient spirit!

Well after a hundred years a building is usually in need of some major repairs and this proved to be the case at Harton. Early in 1980 it became apparent that the roof of the tower was leaking, and that the water which had been entering through it was causing a certain amount of rot in the timbers which support the lead-covered pyramid-roof. Our architect told us that the lead needed stripping, recasting and relaying and that the parts of the roof-timbers which had been rotten would have to be cut out and replaced. This meant an expenditure of something like five thousand pounds, no small sum to raise in a hamlet of less than fifty people. Nevertheless, the people who attended the church, together with others who did not but who were well-disposed towards it, were determined that we must do what we could to raise the money required and accordingly we all met one evening at a nearby farmhouse, home of one of the churchwardens, to discuss how the money-raising might be done. That evening we planned a whole series of events, one of which – perhaps inevitably – was to be a flower festival. It was to be held the following August, the time when we have most visitors in the area. We were lucky in that a very keen and experienced flower-arranger, Mrs Sadie Timms, had recently retired to Wenningham. She agreed to organise the flowers and since the church was small, she said that with the help of some of her floral friends she would be able to put together all the arrangements we would require. Other ladies undertook to organize refreshments in the gardens of the old Parsonage and a produce stall in the churchyard, whilst for my part I undertook to ask the headmaster of the local primary school to provide children's flower-paintings which we could put up on the church walls.

The time of the flower festival came round. Sadie and her friends spent most of the day before its opening doing their arrangements and when I arrived in the mid-evening to put up the flower-paintings, most of them were getting ready to leave, having given the flowers a final spray and put all their spare flowers and foliage in buckets of water beneath the tower. By the time the last of the children's paintings had been fixed in place only Sadie herself was still working. She said that she could finish her final arrangement, a huge mass of red gladioli and golden dahlias placed along the foot of the chancel screen, in ten minutes and that she thought she might as well stay and complete it. It wasn't worth coming back to do it next morning; she had got some shopping to do and then she would come out to Harton just before lunch to see that everything was alright. I must not wait, she said, she had got her car and she had arranged with the man at the old Parsonage who holds the key to lock the church up later on. And so, having complimented her on the appearance of the church and said good-night I returned home.

Next morning I went out to Harton fairly early. I suppose it was about eight-thirty. I wanted to check that everything was ready for the opening at ten o'clock and also I wanted to take out the programmes which I had only finished duplicating late the night before. To my surprise, the church door was open and on entering I found Sadie still working on her red and gold arrangement beneath the screen. I expressed surprise. Hadn't she after all been able to finish it the previous evening? Well no, she replied, in what struck me as being a slightly embarrassed, sheepish manner. Well – something had happened which had made her a little nervous . . . and it had been getting dark, so she thought she would go home and come back again this morning. I was even more surprised because Sadie, like most of the really keen flower-arrangers I have met is a lady with considerable force of character, not at all the kind of person one thinks of as being nervous.

So naturally I asked her what it was that had alarmed her. Whatever had happened?

'Well,' she replied, 'About five minutes after you'd gone, I was kneeling down putting some more leaves into the bottom of this arrangement – I'd noticed that the container was showing – when I heard the sound of the door-handle being turned. I stood up, thinking that it must be you, come back to remind me of something, and naturally I turned round and looked towards the door . . . but though the sound of the handle being turned was followed by the sound of the door opening – you know what a squeaky sound church doors make – yet the door just wasn't moving. I could see quite clearly that it was firmly shut, just as you'd left it. And then I realised that these sounds, and there could be no possible doubt as to what they were, weren't really coming from where the door is at the back of the church; they seemed to be coming from up in the chancel, the other side of the screen from where I was standing. But I know it sounds ridiculous and you won't believe me, because there isn't a door up there, is there?' No, I replied, there isn't. But I added under my breath, At least there isn't now. And I certainly did believe her.

# 12

# The Black Velvet Cap

I have a friend called Timothy Rouse. He is a young unmarried priest and he usually comes to stay with me for a week or so in the Summer as part of his holidays. Last year he wrote and said he would like to stay for a certain week in August, but when I looked in my diary I saw that I had booked my own Summer holiday for that particular week and the one following. I wrote to tell him this, but said that he would be most welcome to use the rectory whilst I was away and that maybe he would be so kind as to say the Eucharist on the Tuesday and Friday whilst he was here. I always try to keep these two services going when I am away on holiday and the daily Eucharist is suspended. A few days later he replied, saying that he wanted to come to Wenningham but could not manage any other week. He would certainly say the two Eucharists for me, but that if I did not mind he would prefer not to stay at the rectory on his own. Could I suggest somewhere else in the village, maybe a small hotel or guest house? – anywhere where there would be a comfortable bed and reasonable food.

I wrote back saying that a small guest house which had recently opened in the High Street might suit him very well. It looked clean, seemed to be reasonably comfortable and people said that the food was plain but good and plentiful. It was called the Priory Gate, for the good reason that it had been formed out of two of the houses which adjoin the great gateway in the High Street, which once led into the domain of the mediaeval priory in Wenningham and now leads into the grounds of the country house built on its site. The two houses, together with all the other property on the East side of the High Street, belong to the Wenningham estate, all of them having once been the buildings which surrounded the outer court of the original priory. The estate had agreed to these particular two houses being joined together, and the work had been carried out by the estate builders. Shortly afterwards my friend wrote back to say that he had booked in at the Priory Gate and was looking forward to his week in the village. He hoped that I would have a good holiday and that next year we would be in Norfolk at the same time.

In due course I went away for my fortnight. I took my car across to France and had a fascinating time looking at the twelfth-century churches of the Auvergne. I returned and a day or two later I phoned Timothy to thank him for taking the two Services for me and to find out how his holiday had gone. We chatted for a while, he telling me about a couple of National Trust properties he had visited in Norfolk, and me telling him about the Romanesque churches I had seen in France. And then I asked him how he had fared at the Priory Gate. He replied that he hoped he would be able to stay at the rectory on his next visit to Wenningham. The food at the guest house had certainly been alright and his room had been clean and comfortable. He had got nothing to complain about in that direction. But he had had a very odd experience. In fact he had been going to phone me himself to tell me about it. That was if I had not already heard: had I seen the agent from the estate since I had been back? Maybe he had mentioned something? No? Well he would tell me what happened. He thought it was the strangest thing he had come across. Whereupon he launched into the story which I will put down as accurately as I can.

It appeared that my friend had gone to bed fairly early on the night of his arrival, at about ten o'clock. He was tired after the long journey driving from Cheshire and like many other busy priests he believes that one of the joys of a holiday is being able both to go to bed and to get up at times which are usually impossible when in the parish. The room he had been given was one which had obviously been affected by the recent alterations, by which the two old houses had been made into one. It had a new doorway and wash-basin and at least two of the walls seemed to have been re-plastered and had probably been inserted to divide the original room. But it retained its two original windows looking out into the High Street. Oak-framed casement windows with diamond-shaped panes, windows he had noticed from the street since they contrasted oddly with the eighteenth century sash-windows in the rest of the house. From these two windows he gauged that his room was situated next to the mediaeval gateway itself.

He was soon asleep and supposed that he had remained asleep for perhaps two or three hours. Then suddenly he woke up – yes, he was quite certain that he had woken up rather than drifted into a dream. Sitting up in bed, he had seen an extraordinary sight. The room was lit by a dim light the source of which was unclear. By that light he saw quite clearly that part of the wall at the side of his bed had disappeared and in the gap a staircase had opened up. Half-way down the staircase a man was standing. The light was dim, but it was sufficient to show that the man appeared to be dressed in clothes which my friend described loosely as Tudor. He could make out that the man was wearing a reddish jacket and that on his head he wore a rather floppy kind of cap, rather, he said, like the Canterbury cap which he teases me for wearing sometimes. It seemed to be made of black velvet. But what struck him most forcibly about this spectacle, he said, was not so much the man's clothes or his stance, but the expression on his face. It was, he said, a look of inexpressible sadness, a sadness such as he had never seen before. The man simply stood on the staircase, perfectly still. He said nothing, there was no movement. Then gradually the dim light by which he was visible began to fade, he became a mere outline, a shadow and then darkness closed in completely. For a few moments Timothy said, he had sat up in bed motionless, too stunned to do anything. And then, seized by a sudden panic, he had reached out for the lamp on his bedside table and switched it on. The flood of light revealed nothing extraordinary. The staircase and its occupant were gone, the wall was just as it had been earlier when he had gone to bed. Nothing was out of place, nothing gave any hint of the apparition which he was perfectly certain he had seen. There is, he said – and I could not argue – a world of difference between what one has seen in a dream and what one has seen with ones eyes and whatever doubts may be raised and entertained by others, we ourselves know quite well how to distinguish the one from the other.

I began to exclaim at this extraordinary incident but Timothy cut me short, saying that this had not been the end of the matter. He had not said anything to the proprietress of the guest house. He imagined, probably correctly, that she would suppose either that he was mad or that he was trying to make a complaint. He had pottered around the village that following morning and then before lunch he had gone across the High Street to have a drink at the Cambridge Arms, a pub almost opposite the Priory Gate. It was fairly quiet in there, not many people were drinking but amongst those who were standing at the bar was John Downey, the recently appointed agent to the Wenningham estate and he and Timothy got into conversation. John asked him if he was on holiday, where he was from and where he was staying. My friend said that he was at the Priory Gate. The agent said that he knew the place well, it was one of the houses that he had to deal with as agent and he gathered that the estate men had spent quite a few weeks working on it not long before he had taken over his present job.

Now John is a very friendly type of person, youngish, good-humoured and easy to talk to. So as the conversation progressed and after a couple of drinks, it so happened that Timothy told him of the strange experience he had had the night before. John, apparently, had smiled and listened with just a trace of amusement and scepticism, but he had not been dismissive. And recognising, I suppose, that Timothy is a sensible, fairly down-to-earth sort of person and was not joking, he showed interest and said he wondered if there ever had been a staircase in that position, a staircase which no longer existed? Well, he said, he knew that the plans for the conversion of the two houses into the present guest house (which, he reminded Timothy, was still basically a mediaeval structure, part of the outer court of the Priory) were in the estate office and if he liked to call some time when the office was open, then they could have a look at them.

My friend had planned to drive down to the coast that afternoon (it is only five miles away from Wenningham) and have a walk on the beach. But, as is not unknown in August, it had begun to drizzle whilst he was having lunch and so he found himself unexpectedly at a loose end. He dozed for a while after the meal, did some reading and then being tired of being indoors and having nothing else to do, he decided mid-afternoon to call at the estate office, which is only just round the corner from the High Street, tucked in the far corner of the Common Place as the Square at Wenningham is known. John happened to be in, the rain having caused him to decide to have an afternoon at his desk. He welcomed Timothy, chatted, and then opening one of the several large cupboards in his room – built-in cupboards painted a uniform grey and containing the mass of papers which accumulate in an estate office. He fetched out a roll of architect's drawings and said that these were the ones relating to the conversion in question; he spread them out on the table, and the two men pored over them. On one of the sheets the architect had drawn plans of the first floor of the building as it had been originally and as he proposed to make it; these plans were drawn side by side. The position of Timothy's room was located immediately on the plans, and yes, even the most casual glance revealed that in the original layout there had indeed been a staircase leading up into that room. Or rather into the space which the room now occupied because formerly it had been a wide landing. Then, when the two houses had been put together, the staircase had simply become superfluous and had been removed thereby allowing the landing to be converted into a further bedroom facing the High Street, whilst the space behind, formerly occupied by the staircase, had been given a floor and made into a bathroom opening off another of the bedrooms.

Timothy, who had never doubted the reality of what he had seen the previous night was not greatly surprised by what the drawings revealed. But John was. Before, he had been politely sceptical, thinking I imagine that it was all just a particularly vivid dream. But now he was intrigued and ready to take the story seriously. He asked Timothy to describe again the appearance of the man who had stood on the staircase, and when the floppy black velvet cap was mentioned he became thoughtful. It seemed, he said, to ring a bell. It sounded familiar. But he couldn't think why . . .

Oh well, Timothy said, he must not take up any more of John's valuable time. He had obviously got a lot of work on his desk. And so having thanked him for showing him the drawings, he said goodbye and began to descend the stairs which lead down from the office to the door opening in to the square. But as he reached the door the agent came down after him, calling to him to wait. Reaching the bottom he said that he had remembered why that black velvet cap seemed to ring a bell. And he explained briefly that although the Wenningham estate had changed hands in both the early seventeenth century and again in the earlier part of the present century, when the Calthorpe family had died out, nevertheless there remained in the priory, rather surprisingly, an almost complete set of portraits of its former owners. These, at the two successive sales, seemed to have stayed in the house. Further, at the Suppression of the Monasteries under Henry VIII the priory lands and buildings had been acquired by a Thomas Suddeley (it was his grandson who had sold the estate to the first of the Calthorpe owners in the 1630s) and the portrait of Thomas Suddeley was the first in that series of portraits. He had reason to know this, John said, because as a genuine sixteenth century portrait it was rare and valuable and the insurance on it – with which he had to deal as agent – was particularly high! Now the point of all this, John continued, was that he was sure that Thomas Suddeley was wearing just the sort of hat in his portrait which Timothy had described, a loose velvet cap. Was Timothy in a hurry? If not, would he like to come over to the priory and see the portrait for himself? The present owners, Mr and Mrs Birbeck, were away in Scotland for the month. The agent naturally had a key and he would be happy to take him across . . . besides the portrait, the house itself was of considerable interest and maybe he would like to see it?

And so, Timothy recounted, they had gone through the wicket in the big gates in the High Street and down the rather muddy drive overhung by tall trees which dripped down rain on them. They reached the front door of the house which John opened. It was dark in the large pillared hall because the shutters had been drawn across the two long windows either side of the door. There were, however, thin lines of light lying across the stone floor, cast from the cracks between the shutters and by these and the light coming from the open front door they walked across to the dining room. The shutters were closed there too, but the agent switched on the lights revealing a long and rather fine room. It had windows on two sides, a wide sideboard recess on the third, and on the fourth side a white marble chimney piece. Around the room, between the windows and elsewhere, hung the remarkable series of family portraits, varying in size as they did in century. Most of them had a small tubular light placed above them and these, since the rest of the lighting in the room was deliberately subdued, made the canvasses stand out and indeed dominate the room. Naturally, the eye

111

was drawn first of all by the large paintings of the eighteenth century Calthorpes, dressed in beautiful silks and satins which the skill of the artist had almost made to rustle. But it was to a much smaller portrait, painted on boards and framed in a plain black surround that John drew his attention. Written on the wooden plate attached to the base of the frame was the name Thomas Suddeley, and to his complete amazement Timothy found himself looking into the face of the same man who had stood on the staircase the night before. He saw before him the reddish jacket, the black velvet cap, and yes, the same look of profound sadness. It seemed extraordinary because, although he had often stayed with me in Wenningham, this was the first time that he had set foot in the Priory, a house which is never open to the public. He knew that he had seen the man in the portrait before and yet he had certainly never seen this portrait before which he now stood.

'So what did you do', I asked. 'What could I do?' was the very natural reply. 'I thanked John for letting me see the portrait in the dining-room and the other main rooms which he kindly showed me afterwards. Then he went back to his office, and because it was still raining I went back again to the guest house and read. But I thought about it a great deal. Most of all I thought about the strange sadness of the man in the portrait and I wondered whether Thomas Suddeley, wherever he may be, had come to recognise the wrong he did in receiving those priory lands, given originally for the service of God and his wrong in turning those priory buildings, built for the glory of

God, into a private house for himself and his family? I reflected too that this house in which I was sitting and in which I'd seen the apparition, that this too was originally one of those priory buildings. And I wondered whether the sadness of Thomas Suddeley could be connected with a recognition he had come to that he had acted wrongly back in the sixteenth century? And so – and you mustn't laugh at this – when next morning I said your Tuesday Eucharist at the Parish church, where I presume Thomas Suddeley must be buried, I offered it for the repose of his soul. I made that my intention, that his soul might be given peace and a place of rest. You might think it sounds a bit silly or romantic, but it just seemed the right thing to do.'

Now each year Mrs Birbeck invites our branch of the Mothers' Union to hold one of its monthly meetings at the Priory and usually this takes place in the big dining room. The table is dismantled, and rows of dining and other chairs are set in place. This annual event took place last year just about two weeks after I had returned from my holiday and shortly after the Birbecks had returned from Scotland. On arrival we were shown into the dining room and you can imagine that after all that Timothy had told me on the telephone I walked straight over to the sixteenth century portrait of Thomas Suddeley as soon as I entered the room. But now it was my turn to be surprised. It certainly could not be said that the man in the painting was smiling. But neither could it be said that he looked particularly sad. Had my friend's prayers had some effect? Had he, in offering that

Eucharist for Thomas Suddeley's soul done just the thing that the man on the staircase had willed him to do? I was still wondering when a voice said 'Ladies, it's time to begin the meeting . . .'.